Motel Gothic

WOL-VRIEY

Burning Bulb
PUBLISHING

Motel Gothic

WOL-VRIEY

Burning Bulb
PUBLISHING

Motel Gothic
By **Wol-vriey**

Burning Bulb Publishing
P.O. Box 4721
Bridgeport, WV 26330-4721
United States of America
www.BurningBulbPublishing.com

Cover concept by Wol-vriey, incorporating images from Pexels.com, Clement Percheron.

First Edition.

Paperback Edition ISBN: 978-1-948278-49-2

Printed in the United States of America.

CHAPTER 1

Dooks, Hicks & Robby

The time was just past a quarter to midnight on a Thursday night. The place was a room in the Sunflower Motel, an establishment on Carver Street in the small Massachusetts town of Raynham.

The room in question was the last one in the rearmost block—the one at the northeast end of the motel. This room had no number as it belonged to Joseph Hicks, the motel's janitor, and as such was never rented out.

It was a large room with attached bathroom and kitchenette, comfortable enough for a middle-aged bachelor without a family, which description perfectly fit Joe Hicks.

Harry Dooks felt very uncomfortable in Hicks's room. And the source of his discomfiture wasn't the unfamiliar surroundings. Though Dooks hadn't been here before, the room was ordinary enough: a medium-sized bed at one end; old couch and two armchairs at the other end, near the TV that hung on the wall.

Hicks was seated in the armchair closest to the TV. Dooks had the chair near the east window, and the room's third human inhabitant, Robby Mayfield, was sprawled out on the couch. Robby half-reeked of booze, but then he nearly always did.

Dooks stared at Robby. Robby was a contender for town drunk. Robby had a flask of whiskey poking from his hip pocket, and his eyes were bloodshot. Without assigning specific blame to any part of his anatomy or clothing, the sonofabitch was unkempt, period.

And yet, Dooks thought, *Robby's the main reason the three of us are here tonight.*

The fourth living occupant of Hicks's room was Robby's dog, Brownie. Brownie looked as rundown and threadbare as Robby did. The dog was male, a brown medium-sized mongrel. Robby had named the dog 'Brownie' because on the day that the stray had taken up

1

permanent residence in his yard, the color of its hair had reminded him of chocolate cake.

Brownie never got much to eat, which was understandable since Robby spent all his money on alcohol. The dog was lying on the floor near the air conditioning unit with his head flat between his forepaws. Every now and then he looked hungrily in their direction and then snapped at the air, biting imaginary flies. Knowing Robby was a useless prospect where satisfying his hunger was concerned, he concentrated his pleading looks solely on Dooks and Hicks.

Well, we needed a dog and here we are!

Dooks saw Hicks was looking at the mutt too. Brownie looked hungrily back at the big man, hoping he'd throw over something edible. But Hicks merely shook his head and grunted back, "Just be patient now, Brownie. You'll have a whole friggin' lot to eat before long."

Brownie hadn't eaten anything for a day; and not by accident; Dooks and Robbie had intentionally starved the dog in preparation for tonight's business.

Hicks had tried to make his voice sound humorous while addressing the dog, but it hadn't come out right. Strain was visible on his broad face, and tonight it wasn't just the toll of his lonely and unsuccessful life making him look and speak like this.

Watching Hicks run a hand through his balding black hair and then flick sweat off of his brow, Dooks felt himself shivering. He knew exactly what Hicks was feeling and he felt it too himself, the butterflies in his belly; the certainty that he might not leave here alive.

He looked down at his hands, gloved in latex even before their arrival at the motel. Robbie's hands were similarly gloved. Hicks had rightly pointed out that since this was his place, it didn't matter if he left fingerprints or not.

This was a night for desperation. *I'm as desperate as they are. I can easily back out—any of us could and the game won't go on—*

"Okay, you guys, last call," Robby interrupted his thoughts, waving a gloved finger in the air. "Any of you motherfuckers wanna back out, this is it. Once we start the game, spellbook says there's no quitting till it's done."

Dooks looked at Hicks. Hicks was sweating profusely now. The sweat wasn't all fear, though. Hicks was sick with something—he'd been very vague as to exactly what his illness was, but from what

Dooks had gathered from Robby, who didn't know much more than himself, Hicks had maybe half a year left to live. On arriving here, Dooks couldn't help noticing the array of medicines on Hicks's nightstand. Also, Hicks's eyes had a nasty yellow tinge to them that didn't speak well of what was happening inside of him.

He's one sick guy, but he's holding up well. He's tough. That much was clear.

Hicks looked defiantly back at both of them and scratched the tip of his bulbous nose. "Listen, guys, I'm damned if I do and damned if I don't. I prefer to take the devil's chance and go out fighting. Let's do this."

That said, he flung a penetrating glance at Dooks, as if daring him to quit.

"I'm in too," Dooks said quietly. "Let's do it."

Robby frowned, suddenly a lot more sober than Dooks ever recalled having seen him. Somewhere nearby a clock struck midnight and in the seconds that followed, it seemed to Dooks as if Death—personified in the form of a young woman (he had no idea why that image of a young woman came to his mind)—was walking nearby.

***

Harry Dooks was thirty-eight years old and as far as he could tell, finished. Two years ago he'd been about to be made a partner in the accounting firm he worked for. And then suddenly, the rug had been yanked out from beneath his feet and he'd been left with nothing.

Dooks had been arrested by the police and charged with helping cook the books for a soft drinks company. It took eighteen months and a court trial before Dooks was cleared of any wrongdoing in the case. But by then the accounting firm had fired him anyway, and his name had become mud in the business world, as his later futile attempts to find work proved.

There actually had been wrongdoing, but Dooks had been made the fall guy. There was big money involved—tens of millions of dollars and a mob money laundering trail that extended all the way from Las Vegas to Wall Street—and Dooks was just a little fish fighting to swim to safety while the financial sharks gnashed their jagged teeth at him.

While Dooks had been on trial for fraud, there had also been an internet smear campaign against him, with paid trolls hinting that he was also a rapist and pedophile. This was all completely untrue, but nowadays the mere suggestion of guilt is often more than enough to crucify the innocent.

These sex-offender accusations had backfired on Dooks in another way. Dooks had a child by an ex-girlfriend; and now, scared that there was some truth to the pedophile allegations, she had sought and gotten sole custody of their eight-year-old daughter.

(At the moment, Harry Dooks, who'd been the most loving daddy imaginable, could only visit his daughter once every three months and then only under strict supervision by CPS.)

Finally, however, Dooks had walked out of court a free man, with five hundred dollars in the bank and twenty thousand dollars left to pay in lawyer's fees. More bankrupt than if he'd spent the last ten years unemployed.

Understandably, his mortgage had been foreclosed during his legal troubles, and he'd lost his house . . . and his car.

When the hammer blow of losing the house had fallen, Dooks had packed up the few things in the house that still legally belonged to him, kissed the memories of the place goodbye, and then walked down three or four streets to Robby Mayfield's place.

Dooks had known Robby since elementary school.

Robby Mayfield now lived in a small bungalow on Raynham's Theresa Road. He'd been in the marines in Iraq but had come back invalided—three bullets in the gut had given him a small disability pension that he spent on booze and hookers. The house had been his grandfather's. Its yard was overgrown with weeds and the neighbors complained constantly that he was lowering property values, but whenever either they or the town authorities came around to air their latest grievances, Robby simply invited them in for drinks.

Robby also didn't have a wife or kids—he'd been divorced for as long as Dooks could remember; which made his pad the ideal place to crash for Dooks, who really had nowhere else to go. After the public so-called 'revelations' about his thievery and sex crimes (all of which had, of course, been spread far and wide via Facebook and YouTube), none of Dooks's friends wanted anything to do with him anymore.

Except for one of them: Robby never paid his phone bill, so his internet never worked. Meaning, there was no way he'd have been following the smear campaign against Dooks.

When Dooks arrived at Robby's, Robby had been passed out drunk on the couch and his dog Brownie, hungry as always, had been doing his unsuccessful best to pry last night's half-eaten burger from his owner's grasp. Dooks had dropped his bags on the living room floor, walked over to the couch, and wincing from the smell of puke on Robby, helped the dog free the burger from Robby's fingers. This act of human-to-canine kindness seemed to eternally mark him as a friend to Brownie.

The dog ran off with the retrieved burger and Dooks, after grimly considering how far down in the world he'd fallen, walked off into Robby's kitchen to see if there was any beer in the fridge.

When Robby woke up, Dooks had told him he'd like to rent a room for a while, handed him three hundred dollars in cash, and then moved into the house's spare room.

Robby had taken the money and, with Brownie in tow, had headed off to the stores to buy booze and dog food.

***

Dooks's slight optimism that his situation might improve given time proved wrong. The internet trolls' smear campaign had ruined him. He'd quickly discovered he had no chance of earning a living in his former profession.

Time had moved on and he'd become old history.

True, he'd been cleared of any wrongdoing in the fraud scandal that had cost him his job, but . . . there were rumors that his exoneration hadn't really been due to his innocence, but rather due to several out-of-court financial settlements, payments to witnesses and aggrieved parties by the accounting firm Dooks had worked for, to protect its reputation.

It was all lies, but Dooks still found himself out in the cold.

Other work? Well, not with him being labelled as both a potential rapist and pedophile; the internet trolls had really made Dooks look as bad as possible in the public eye. Now even Walmart and Dunkin' refused to hire him.

So he'd worked on a few farms, dug a few ditches . . . And then, just when he'd begun thinking about sticking a gun in his mouth and ending things, Robby had suggested that they play the Devil's Coin Game.

***

And so we wound up here tonight, Dooks thought, once more looking down at his gloved hands. *It seemed such a joke when Robby told me about the book he'd found in his cousin the supposed witch's house . . .*

That night a week ago, it really had seemed a joke. Rain pouring down . . . Robby staggering into the house with a bag of beer in one hand, while Brownie dashed in past his legs and then shook himself dry all over the carpet . . . Robby pulling a book out from his coat and then drunkenly telling Dooks, "I just found the solution to our problems—it's called the Devil's Coin Game."

The book lay on the coffee table now. Necromantica Vol. 2333. It was a slim, creepy thing bound in pale skin. Dooks hated touching it. All of them did—there was just something unnatural about that book, something horrible.

That first night, immediately I touched it, I knew it was the real deal . . . otherwise, I'd have simply walked away from all this. 'Cos what we're about to do is the true definition of madness. We're really about to attempt a magic ritual that involves human sacrifice. At least the dog'll have a full belly.

He looked over at the dog. Brownie, a stoic trooper trained by past days of dietary abstinence when Robby had either drunk or whored away all their food money, was staring hungrily at a fly on the wall that was too high for him to reach.

The dog's owner, however, was much more animated, waving his gloved hands at Dooks and Hicks. Tonight Robby was an odd combination of intoxication and exhilaration. He appeared too drunk to care that he might soon be dead. Dooks had to admire his spirit.

Dooks and Robby were the same height and weight, but there the similarities ended. Robby had untidy long dark hair and a badly trimmed beard; badly trimmed because he always had a hooker friend cut it for him instead of visiting the barber like everyone else did. He described his blue eyes as 'true-American red, white and blue ones,' because they were invariably bloodshot from his drinking.

Dooks himself had short dirty-blonde hair, but he at least tried to shave and bath regularly and dress neatly. Even though a good look in his gray eyes revealed that he was slowly going to the dogs too, he was fighting against his personal decline until the bitter end.

"Well, seeing as no one's gotten cold feet," Robby said. "I guess we'd better get on with playing the Devil's Game." He laughed coldly. "Besides, my dog's getting' hungry."

"Yeah, let's get it over with," Hicks said in a mean voice. "If I'm gonna die, I don't wanna first die of anticipation."

Hicks was a big man. Big as in both tall and fat; much like the biker types who were always pulling into Rudy's Truck Stop, the inn/drinking establishment up near the I-495 interstate overpass, when Dooks and Robby went drinking there. To Dooks's mind, Hicks would fit in perfectly with that rowdy crowd. About the only 'little' parts of Hicks were his small black mustache and his tiny black eyes.

Dooks didn't really know Hicks. The big man was an old drinking buddy of Robby's. However, the Devil's Coin Game required three players, and down at the bottom of life's barrel himself, Dooks hadn't known anyone else desperate enough to gamble away their life on the toss of a coin.

But Robby had come up with Hicks, the Sunflower Motel's janitor.

The same thing went for their current location. Though Robby's house was isolated, they couldn't hold the ritual there. It didn't matter what time of the day or night it was, there was always someone likely to stop by Robby's place—some drunk looking for a free beer or somewhere to crash, or a hooker either looking for business or coming to collect her money for last time.

Too risky. So they'd decided to use Hicks's room at the motel. Dooks had suggested their wearing gloves . . .

Using the motel wasn't exactly foolproof either, as there were always folks checking in and out; and at odd times too. But the three men would be holding their ritual at midnight, when they expected much less human traffic. And besides, Hicks's room was in the back block anyway, the rooms of which generally weren't let out unless all those in the front two blocks were taken. And from what Hicks had told them on their arrival—tonight was a slow night, very few guests had checked in.

The window drapes were of course tightly shut.

Dooks and Robby had also taken the precaution of arriving at the Sunflower Motel through the surrounding woods at its rear, so no one would notice either their arrival or departure.

"Just lookin' at that magic book give me the willies," Hicks said with a shudder when Robby crouched beside the coffee table. "But there's no denyin' it's the real deal." The big man was dressed in faded pants and a wifebeater and was sweating way more than one would expect considering the mild weather.

Robby picked up the skin-bound volume from the coffee table, waved it at them, and then put it down again beside a large paper bag. Then he got out his flask of whiskey from his hip pocket.

"Sorry, guys, I need a little Dutch courage before we do this," he said with a smile and then unscrewed the top of the flask and took a long pull.

"Okay, no more bullshit," Robby said after putting the flask away. He opened up the paper bag and began taking out its contents. First came out three knives, then next a roll of duct tape, and last of all a quarter.

Robbie handed the knives around. They were identical survival knives from Cashstretch, advertised on TV as having an 'unbluntable razor-sharp edge.'

As Dooks's fingers touched the weapon's cold metal, he felt disconnected from reality. He glanced at Hicks; the big man was staring at his knife like it was a road accident. He seemed both terrified of it and yet unable to look away.

Robby picked up the quarter from the coffee table. "Okay, gentlemen, let's play the Devil's Coin Game."

CHAPTER 2

Mandy & Dewdrop

Riding shotgun in the rented black Honda Accord, Dewdrop sighed and fanned herself with her short fingers.

"Darling," she told Mandy in a mock theatrical voice, "a lovely night like this would be much better spent making love in a soft bed."

Mandy Cherry was about turning the car into the driveway of the Sunflower Motel. She stomped the brake pedal; half to get a look at their destination; half to reply her partner. Dewdrop was smiling.

"I know what you mean," Mandy replied. "But unfortunately, we've gotta earn a living, right?"

"You took the words right out of my mouth, girl, "Dewdrop said, pursing her lips in mock sadness while she spoke.

Dewdrop was a short young woman with long blonde hair. Mandy Cherry was taller, slimmer and had short black hair. Both were dressed similarly, in black leather jackets, dark denim skirts and black leggings that ended in black boots. The main reason neither of them would be mistaken for goths was their lack of makeup.

Mandy giggled. "Honey, as much as I would rather at this moment be holed up somewhere with my mouth on your pussy, we've a murder to commit."

Dewdrop sighed. "Yeah. Well, maybe afterwards. Killing this greedy bitch shouldn't take too long."

Mandy nodded her reply. She shared her girlfriend's optimism. Tenebra clearly didn't suspect anything was amiss. When they'd phoned her earlier, she'd given them her motel room number without any fuss and told them she'd expect them at around midnight.

Mandy checked the dashboard clock; the time was now a quarter past midnight.

She hadn't missed the anticipation of the coming bloodletting in Dewdrop's voice. Dewdrop got off on violence more than Mandy did.

For Mandy, killing people was just a way to earn a living. She'd always had a sharp mind, but had been unable to apply herself to reading and getting good grades. She also didn't want to spend her life working in a Jewish deli like her mother.

***

Twenty-two year old Mandy Cherry had first killed someone two years ago.

While drinking at a male friend's house, he had bitterly complained to her about how much easier his life at work would be if a certain annoying co-worker was dead, and how he really wished he could hire someone to do the dirty deed—without being caught, of course.

Mandy had offered to do the job for him. For twenty grand. Her friend had jokingly agreed; he'd doubted she'd dare go through with it.

But Mandy had been dead serious. She'd just gotten through a stint as a bar waitress and had hated the way the male patrons kept staring at her body. And seeing as she was an unapologetic lesbian, she knew she couldn't work as a prostitute either. The mere thought of men penetrating her body made her feel like killing them all.

But she needed a guaranteed way to earn a living. And here was a chance to get paid good money.

So Mandy had stalked her friend's co-worker, and two weeks later, had slit his throat just after he'd left a bar at night. Then she'd quickly pulled out her cellphone and taken a picture of the dying man, which she'd forwarded to her friend along with her bank account details.

There had been no argument at all about paying up. Her friend's only request was that she wait a few months for the money, so the police didn't get suspicious.

After that first kill, it had been easier. Her first client had told another trusted friend about Mandy and she began to get regular murderous work.

Mandy had met Dewdrop on her fifth hit. A man had asked her to kill the drug dealer who'd gotten his daughter strung out on junk.

Mandy had taken her time to set the hit up and then, posing as a junkie buyer, had carried it out. And everything had gone well, right up to the point when, after stabbing the drug dealer five or six times in the neck and belly and leaving him with his guts spread out all over his bed, she'd turned to leave his run-down apartment and had pulled up short in alarm.

There had been a short blonde girl standing in the doorway to the bathroom. The girl had a look of intense surprise on her face. She didn't seem scared though; that was the odd thing.

It took Mandy a few seconds to realize that the young woman had watched her kill her target and had been masturbating while doing so. She was wearing just a long pink tee shirt. Her large thighs were wet with female juice, and even if they hadn't been, she was still rubbing herself and sighing in pleasure.

The girl's presence presented a clear complication for Mandy. Kill her or not?—that was the problem.

Then the girl had pulled her fingers out of her sex and begun laughing, laughing and pointing at the dead man as if he was the funniest thing she'd ever seen. She laughed so much that Mandy had begun thinking she was crazy.

"I've always wanted to kill that fucker," the girl told Mandy when she'd calmed a little. "I just never had the guts to go through with it. I was always scared of getting caught and going to jail."

"Who the fuck are you?" Mandy had asked her.

"Name's Dewdrop." She'd spat at the dead man. "That's my dad there. He's been fucking me without my consent since I was a teenager. Most times in my ass. At the moment my asshole is wide enough to stick a beer can inside."

Then, still clearly unafraid, she'd stuck out her wet hand at Mandy. "Hey, I like you. Let's be friends. And you're pretty too; I wanna eat your pussy. After what that asshole put me through, I'm turning lesbian anyway . . . and you, don't bother denying it—you have dyke stamped all over you."

Mandy decided not to kill her but to fuck her instead. There was something both cute and endearingly crazy about the other girl.

And just to prove how crazy she could be, next thing Mandy knew, Dewdrop was pulling her down onto the messy bed on which her dead father lay and inviting her to lick her dripping vagina.

They'd been together since then. Considering Mandy's line of business, Dewdrop had been a natural recruit. She'd taken to paid murder like a fish to water.

***

The Sunflower Motel was mostly invisible from the road, courtesy of a line of trees that bordered Carver Street at this point. This of course had the advantage that Mandy and Dewdrop's car couldn't be clearly seen by those inside the enclosure.

The moon was bright tonight and created a desire for romance and drama in both of the murderous young lovers.

After leaning over the gearshift to plant a kiss on Dewdrop's lips, Mandy put the Honda back in motion and swept down the motel driveway.

"Not much of a place," she said with a scowl as the motel buildings came into clear view.

"It's okay," Dewdrop disagreed. "Better than a lot of dives I roomed in while travelling with my dad as a teen. Hey, kill the damn headlights."

Mandy frowned and did so. She realized she'd gotten carried away by the lovely night. Such distractions were dangerous.

The motel was built in five sections. A middle two-story building with a 'Sunflower Motel' sign across the upper balcony and 'Reception' sign over the front entrance was flanked on the right by a restaurant. The motel proper was situated to the left of the reception house; a complex of three long buildings.

Mandy swung the Honda left, onto the front parking lot. Tenebra, the woman they were here to kill, was rooming in Room 13, in the middle block.

The reception lights were on and a glance through the glass double-doors revealed a bearded middle-aged guy sitting at the reception desk, not noticing them because he was watching TV.

"It really doesn't pay to be greedy," Dewdrop remarked as they left the reception house behind and began passing the cars parked outside the rooms in the front rental block. "Petra Velli is paying us two hundred grand to off Tenebra—exactly the same amount that Tenebra is blackmailing her for. How ironic. Why not just pay Tenebra off?"

Mandy shrugged. "The difference is that in our case, we won't be back for more money when this payment runs out." She laughed. "Except of course, if Petra has another ex-girlfriend she wants to snuff out."

Dewdrop joined in her laughter. "Maybe the old cow will keep it in her pants from now on. Too much chance of her husband finding out what happened during her trip to the Big Apple."

Mandy nodded. "Maybe she will. According to Petra, this was the first time she'd stepped out of line since her marriage. And he was out of the country at the time."

Petra Velli was married to ruthless Boston mobster Marko Velli. Her 'sexual indiscretion' with Tenebra was certain to result in major embarrassment for Marko in mob circles, if as she'd threatened, Tenebra uploaded online the photos she'd taken of herself and Petra in bed.

So, Petra, terrified of what her husband would do to her if that happened, had hired Mandy and Dewdrop to do damage limitation.

"*Really?*" Dewdrop scoffed, flapping her fingers out of the car window. "And you believed that? Petra didn't strike me as being the most truthful woman in the world."

"Yeah. Maybe she was telling the truth that this was her first time muff-diving, but I'm sure that doesn't apply to men too. Petra Velli has slut written all over her. Even while crossing her living room, she moves her hips like she's fucking someone."

"I think she spends most of her boring marriage finding new ways to get into sexual mischief."

Mandy's skeptical laughter was cut off when a brunette walked around the end corner of the front block. On the woman's unexpected appearance, Mandy instantly forgot their manizing employer and focused on the problem this woman created.

For one thing, she couldn't have appeared at a worse place, just as Mandy had been about to turn the corner. The lights were on in several rooms in the motel's front block, and not wishing to attract any attention to their passage with their headlights off, Mandy had been driving at very moderate speed along the front block, and had slowed even more to make the turn.

And once the woman had appeared, Mandy had also instinctively stomped on the brake so as not to run into her. The last thing they needed tonight was to be part of a motor accident.

From Mandy's point of view, that was. While Dewdrop took a very lax approach to being a hitwoman, Mandy never let down her guard. She had always worried about police detection of their activities; and since hooking up with Dewdrop was now worrying for two people.

And aside from CCTV cameras and leaving fingerprints or an ID trail, the other primary way the cops found out who'd murdered someone was by witness testimony.

In this case CCTV cameras weren't really an issue. The two she'd so far noticed were focused on filming the doorways along the front block. Besides, even if the cameras captured their Honda's registration number, the vehicle couldn't be traced to either of them. They'd rented it with fake ID, courtesy of a trans friend of theirs who specialized in such things. They'd also been well disguised while picking up the vehicle.

But eyewitnesses? That was another thing. Mandy felt the beginning of a deep frustration. *Is this gonna be another of those hits that need to be postponed? Petra won't be pleased.*

"She looks like a hooker," Dewdrop pointed out, gesturing at the woman outside the car.

Now that she was over her surprise at the woman's unexpected appearance, Mandy took a good look at her and saw that her girlfriend was right. Well illuminated in one of the front block's security lights, the brunette, who was now walking around the hood of the Honda, had to be a prostitute. The woman, who seemed to be in her mid-thirties, wore just a short blue party dress that barely covered her hips, and out of the top of which her large breasts bulged, and, visible as she stepped fully past the hood of the car, blue high heels.

Other than that she carried a small red handbag. Mandy figured all she had in the purse were condoms. She was also heavily made up.

She was solid enough, and yet, possibly because of how unexpectedly she'd appeared in front of the car, there also seemed to be something ethereal about her. Like she didn't really belong here at the motel.

"What we gonna do 'bout her?" Dewdrop asked. "Running into her definitely wasn't part of tonight's plan."

"We'll wait and see if she walks past us. The house light is in her eyes, so she can't really see into the car except she steps close to us."

But that was exactly what was happening. Almost before Mandy had finished speaking, the brunette was standing by the driver's door and peeking down into the Honda with her hair dangling down to tickle Mandy's left arm.

Mandy cursed herself for stopping; and then she wondered why she'd not just driven past the woman and damned the consequences.

At the very worst, this hooker would have just remembered the car make and its registration number. But now, Mandy realized the brunette could see their faces; the security light was spilling through the car too, illuminating both the dashboard and the vehicle's two inhabitants.

"Hi, girls, you looking for some fun?" the prostitute asked them with a seductive smile. Up close she was even more heavily made up than she'd first seemed to be. Mandy couldn't even tell if she was pretty or not.

"No, we aren't looking for your sort of fun," Mandy curtly replied the prostitute. "We're just going to our room to get some sleep."

The hooker wasn't to be dissuaded however. To buttress her selling points, she placed her palms against the sides of her breasts and pressed them together. She wasn't wearing a bra and her generous bosom now lay on the window's edge like two overstuffed pillows. "Listen, you two look like nice girls, so I'll do you a special discount rate for a threesome. Two hundred for an hour or eight hundred for the whole night. So, how 'bout it?"

Instead of replying the proposition, Mandy shut her eyes and gripped the steering wheel hard. Wow! Suddenly she felt creeped out by the hooker. She couldn't have explained to anyone how she felt; she didn't properly understand her fear. But suddenly, meeting with this brunette prostitute here tonight was as undesirable as running into the devil in a dark alley in a ghost town.

She sat shivering with her eyes closed, wondering what was wrong with her, while the hooker continued her proposition with Dewdrop:

"Hey, honey, your friend here seems a bit shy. But you look like you'll enjoy what I'm selling; so I'll let you convince her. Darling, I'll eat both your pussies so fine, you'll both swear off men forever."

"Okay, bitch, you're on," Dewdrop agreed. "But you'd better be as good as you claim, or I'll stomp all your teeth in."

"I'll be the best fuck you'll ever have. After me, you won't mind dying." She spoke the word 'dying' with a breathy exhalation that made it sound sexy. "So should I climb into the car?"

"Not yet. You need to wait for us."

Mandy felt the shift of the prostitute's body next to her, the adjustment of her lush contours; sniffed a flow of rose-tinged perfume; heard the disappointment in her voice.

She opened her eyes. The prostitute's face now expressed her satisfaction that she'd successfully sold herself, but also carried the worry caused by this proposed delay in getting down to business. "You don't want me to get in the car now?" Then she giggled. "Or maybe you're kinky, you wanna do it outside, on the hood. Well, we can. I don't mind. I don't think anyone's checked into these last three rooms, so . . . so long as you ain't a screamer when you come, we can . . ."

Dewdrop shook her head at her. "No, that's not it. You just can't get in the car right now. Not now. We're here to visit my uncle and he's a fire-n-brimstone preacher—real uptight. We're already hours late to see him and if he sees you too, he's gonna think the worst. But once we're done there—won't take longer than fifteen minutes—we'll be back for ya."

"But your friend just said you girls are rooming here," the prostitute countered.

"She lied. Listen, wait for us and we'll hire you for the whole night."

"Alright, I'll wait," the prostitute agreed. "But I always get paid in advance. I never joke with my money."

"Yeah, yeah, I'm familiar with business ethics. I've sold my ass too, you know."

At this point Mandy managed to rejoin the conversation. "If we don't swear off guys after having sex with you, do we get a refund?"

The prostitute rolled her eyes. "No, honey, you simply pay me to try to convince you again."

And on that wisecrack she sauntered off around the rear of the car, with her heels clicking on the concrete, calling back over her shoulder: "I'll be down by the reception."

Mandy watched her go in the rearview. She couldn't help admiring the way the woman was working for her money, shaking her hips with emphasis as if she had gold between her legs.

Maybe her pussy really is a goldmine, she mused. *Maybe that tramp will be the best fuck either of us have ever had, better than each other even.*

"Too bad we're gonna have to kill her, huh?" Dewdrop said.

Mandy took her eyes off the rearview, looked over at Dewdrop, and nodded. "Yeah . . . but there's something real odd about her."

"What you talking about?"

Mandy shook her head. "I can't put it in words. But after meeting her, I almost feel like calling this hit off, driving well away from here, and never looking back."

Dewdrop frowned. "And what about the money? You're forgetting we've already spent half of our advance payment."

Mandy grimaced. "Yeah, I know, that's why I said 'almost.' I know we can't quit now." She pointed ahead. "It makes no sense to do so. Tenebra is just around the corner."

She looked once more in the rearview mirror. The hooker had vanished now; maybe into the reception house if she regularly worked the motel, or maybe she'd found someone to sell a quick blowjob to while waiting for her more lucrative two female clients to return.

"I feel almost like I just spoke to a ghost," Mandy said. "Like I had chills down my spine when she was leaning inside the car. I felt totally . . . Ugh!"

Dewdrop leaned over and kissed Mandy on the cheek. "I can understand why you feel creeped out by that hooker. She was totally flesh and blood, but she really did look spooky. Did you notice she was wearing enough makeup for four people?"

Mandy nodded and then laughed. "Oh, I'm just being silly." She eased her foot off the Honda's brake pedal and turned the vehicle around the end of the front block. "Come on, baby, let's go kill that greedy bitch Tenebra. And then we'll pick up the hooker and kill her too, so she can't rat on us to the cops. A bitch like that'll likely have a rap sheet a mile long; she'll start singing even before they get her to the police station."

"But we'll only kill her after sampling her wares, of course," Dewdrop replied with a lewd grin on her face. "It won't hurt at all if we enjoy her before we kill her."

"Nah, it won't hurt a bit—not us anyway."

"I'm thinking . . ."

" 'Bout what, darling?"

"Maybe we can make a deal with the hooker. We won't kill her if she's so good in the sack that she really does make us abandon sex with men forever."

"But we're *lesbians*, we already dislike sex with men."

"Yeah. Too bad for her. We'll just enjoy her and leave her remains for the pigs to clean up." That settled, they drove to the second block for their appointment with Tenebra.

CHAPTER 3

Dooks, Hicks & Robby

The tension in Hicks's room would need a chainsaw to dissipate. The Devil's Card Game had begun.

Each with their gleaming and razor-sharp survival knife placed beside them, Dooks, Hicks, and Robby sat facing the coffee table. Their faces were strained. Each man knew his life was on the line here.

Brownie the dog watched expectantly from his desolate corner of the motel room,

Dooks grimaced when Robby picked up the Necromantica spellbook from where it lay beside him on the couch. Robby had already opened up the spellbook to the relevant page and used the quarter to wedge it open. Now, holding coin in left hand and summoning book in right, he squinted for a moment at the text and then read out:

"Eb lliw sevil owt, emag slived eht yalp lliw ew. . . ."

"What's that mean?" Hicks asked uneasily. "Sounds like you've got gravel in your mouth."

Robby shushed him and went on: "S'deecorp eht paer ot niamer lliw eno, tiefrof . . . "

Hicks looked even more uneasy as Robby finished up the spell. Dooks looked at the big man's sick and worried face; he knew that right about now he himself looked just as sick and worried.

There was no doubt about it; they were messing with dangerous forces here. As Robby recited the guttural words from the spellbook, Dooks felt as if invisible hands were rolling back the fabric of reality.

He nervously glanced around. To his relief the motel room still looked the same. He'd almost expected to find they'd been translated to some flaming nether realm with evil spirits lurking everywhere.

But, though the motel room looked the same, it didn't feel the same. Even Brownie recognized that. The mongrel had retreated from his former place. At the moment Brownie looked like he was trying to force himself through the wall and outside. Then the dog whined softly and covered his eyes with his forepaws.

"Well, hell heard us for sure," Dooks heard Robby say, so he turned back to look at the others.

"What'cha talking 'bout?" Hicks was asking.

Robby smirked a little drunkenly and flipped the quarter to Hicks. "Proof of success, Joe."

Hicks snatched the coin out of the air and looked at it. Dooks watched his eyes widen as he turned the coin over and over, and then with his eyes really wide, he tossed the coin to Dooks. Then, letting out a massive whoosh of breath that seemed to deflate him, Hicks sank back into his chair and shut his eyes.

Dooks examined the coin and immediately got the gist. The coin was no longer the same. Dooks was so surprised at its transformation that he almost dropped it. The spellbook had required an ordinary coin—any minted coin would do. The text had cryptically stated that the devil would 'furnish his own currency'; but of course, neither Robby nor Dooks had understood what that meant.

But now Dooks understood what it meant. This coin he now held had a demon's head—complete with horns and forked tongue—on one side, and a curled tail that ended in an arrowhead on the other side.

Dooks tried to apply rationality to this transformation and failed. *I'm the one who gave Robby that quarter and it's been lying there inside that book on the coffee table in plain view of all three of us since he took it out of the bag. Yeah, I did turn away to look at the dog . . . but Hicks was watching Robby all that time and he didn't notice a switch*—he looked from the coin he held to Hicks, who was just reviving from his slump—*so I guess, it's exactly like Robby says: the coin transformed in his hand as proof of our success in starting the ritual.*

The coin felt normal to Dooks; it didn't appear supernatural or anything like that; it was just a silver coin. But he admitted he might be wrong, any odd sensation coming from the coin might be dulled by the latex covering his fingers. But the gloves were essential protection. Like using a condom on your manhood—you didn't feel as much of your lady friend as you deserved to, but you were a hell of a lot safer for that slight loss of pleasure. So too Dooks figured it was in this case, though he doubted the devil's currency he was holding could transmit any sort of physical infection.

He flicked the coin back to Robby, who caught it and then began turning it over between his fingers.

"So, hell really has heard us," Hicks said. "Well, in that case, gentlemen, I guess it's time to give 'em what they want, and get what we want in return," The big man seemed completely recovered from his earlier shock. He was still sweating though, but clearly not from fear. The look of determination in his eyes chilled Dooks, who was still unsettled by that earlier sensation of reality being peeled away from around them. And Hicks's voice had sounded hopeful. Seeing that transformed coin must have reassured him that he might soon be well again, with whatever fatal ailment was eating him up purged from his system.

A sudden loud scratching noise, like the movement of rats in a wall, made Dooks glanced quickly at the dog. To his surprise, Brownie wasn't in his previous corner and so Dooks looked around for him. Brownie was up on his haunches and scratching desperately at Hicks's door, like he wanted to get out. Dooks knew the dog didn't want to go pee; he'd already done so on their way over. And he also knew that the dog didn't want to leave because he was so desperately hungry.

The mutt feels it too! He knows that at this moment, this particular motel room is a very bad place to be. Don't worry, Brownie, you aren't in any danger here.

Once more Dooks looked back at the others. Hicks was scowling at the devil's coin as Robby held it up.

"I know it's illogical," Hicks said, "but that demon face is so ugly, I doubt I'm gonna have any luck allying myself with it."

Robby looked inquiringly at Dooks.

Dooks stared evenly back at the drunk, but couldn't help wondering if perhaps Hicks was right and the demon face on the coin signaled bad luck for each of them.

But really, it's all the same in the end. The coin won't ever land on its edge. It'll be either heads of tails. That's even-Steven. Except of course, if the devil is rigging his own game; and with his reputation, who's to say he isn't?

"As for me," Robby said while waving Dooks's transformed quarter at Hicks, "I feel something real comforting about this damn devil face. Reminds me of my platoon sergeant in Iraq. Sonofabitch was ugly as Satan's butt, but had a heart of gold—least he did till the damn towelheads blew him sky-high, so sky-high the vultures must've thought we were serving them lunch and just snatched his scraps out of the air. We didn't even find enough of him to bury."

"Git on with it, wilya?" Hicks growled at him. "You should've fucking died over in Iraq; then your drunk ass wouldn't be here pissing me off."

Robby nodded. "Calm down, you fat sonofabitch. I'm just trying to delay my death, that's all. Or maybe it's one of you guys that'll be unlucky." Then he shrugged and picked up both his survival knife and the roll of duct tape. "Okay, now remember how we play this: After we gag ourselves with the duct tape, we'll each take turns with flipping the coin." He stopped speaking and looked pointedly first at Hicks and then at Dooks, and for the first time tonight Dooks read the worry in his eyes. "We'll go clockwise, meaning first coin toss is Hicks's, second is Harry's, and I go last. You can either stop the coin on the back of your hand and show us the result, or let it land on the floor or the coffee table; don't matter which, so long as the three of us see a clean, unmistakable result. If the results of the coin toss are two heads to one tail, or vice versa, whoever is in the minority automatically loses and becomes our sacrifice to Satan."

Dooks watched Hicks shift uneasily at this reminder. He also began wondering how Robby, who was clearly quite drunk and who should by all rights be slurring his speech, was able to string all of this together and make logical sense of it to boot. But then Robby had also managed to read out the spell without messing up the words.

Of course, Dooks wasn't certain of this last and felt a sudden thrill of panic: *I should have insisted on reading the spell, and not let Robby do it. It's not even English, what the hell do we know that he read? For all that Hicks and I know, drunk Robby may have completely fucked up the spell he just cast and put us at the devil's mercy. Maybe we're already down in hell, even . . . one step outside of this motel room and there's demons waiting to torment us for all eternity.* He managed to calm himself. *But . . . well, the coin did alter . . . so I guess he got most of the words right.*

". . . And of course, if it comes up either heads or tails all three times," Robby was saying, "we're gonna cancel that round and play again, until someone loses." He frowned. "We all clear on this?"

"Yeah, let's do it," Hicks said.

Robby looked at Dooks and then picked up the duct tape and peeled off a long strip of it, which he cut off from the reel with his knife.

"Seems weird to be doing this to oneself," he said. "It's almost like I'm kidnapping myself." Then he slapped the strip of tape over his mouth and pressed it securely down. Then he threw the roll of tape to Hicks, who after studying the silver tape for a moment, peeled off a similar strip and did the same as Robby had. Then he in turn threw the roll of tape over to Dooks.

Gagging themselves like this was wholly Dooks's idea, although Hicks didn't know that. But Dooks had pointed out to Robby that if they were going to murder one of their number, it was best to prevent whoever it was from being able to scream for help once they discovered they'd lost the deadly gamble.

And that includes me, of course, Dooks thought as he slapped the duct tape over his own lips. *Right now my life doesn't seem to mean much to me; but what about if I lose the coin toss? A sixty-six percent chance of winning is better than fifty-fifty odds, but each of us has a thirty-three percent chance of losing too.*

He decided there was no point thinking about it. He had done his best to prepare for the few eventualities that he could. He'd thought of their secret arrival, the gloves . . . the duct tape. The rest resided firmly in the hands of God or Fate.

Robby was holding up the coin, and was looking at them both inquisitively, while mumbling an inaudible question through his taped-over mouth.

Hicks nodded. Dooks nodded. Even though he was now too conscious of his reduced chances of survival to turn and look at Brownie again, Dooks was aware that the dog had given up his attempts at the door and had settled down to watch proceedings and hope someone would soon remember to feed him.

While all three men held their knives at the ready, Robby once more tossed the Devil's coin over to Hicks and nodded.

Hicks took a deep breath and flipped the coin.

***

Once out of Hicks's hand, the coin spun in the air; and Dooks had the impression that it was spinning slower than a normal coin would. He didn't think time really slowed down, but he imagined he counted several heartbeats before Hicks finally smacked the coin down on the back of his left hand.

Without any preamble, Hicks showed the others the result. Tails.

Dooks examined Hicks's face. The big man seemed pleased with the result. Dooks remembered that Hicks had emphatically stated that he didn't like the demon head engraved on the coin.

Hicks nodded to Dooks and then tossed the devil's coin his way.

This time Dooks couldn't help but study the coin for a few moments, switching its faces around in his palm as if to reassure himself that it was just a piece of metal that wasn't alive in any way.

No, it didn't really just slow down in midair. And yes, this damn demon head is very creepy. I don't blame Hicks for getting nervy 'bout it.

Hicks coughed. Dooks looked at him again and almost laughed. Hicks had an impatient look on his face that seemed to say: "Get on with it. What'cha tryin' to do, kill me with suspense?"

Dooks tried apologizing for the delay, but the duct tape over his mouth immediately reminded him of why it was in place. So he nodded silently to Hicks instead.

Dooks flipped the coin. This time too, it seemed to spin slower than a normal coin would—he was now certain of it. But that no longer bothered him, because in the interim after the coin left his hand, it occurred to him that if the coin turned up 'tails' like it had for Hicks, he'd be automatically saved for this round, regardless of what Robby cast.

The very worst that can happen then is a replay . . .

Dooks was so intent on this thought that his attempt to slap the coin down on the back of his hand like Hicks had done failed and it instead dropped to the rug. It bounced once and then came to a stop beneath the coffee table.

All three men got down on their knees to see what it showed.

Heads. Well, I'm not saved yet.

He saw that Robby was touching his head, and wondered why. Then he understood that Robby wanted their agreement that Dooks had gotten 'heads.' He nodded back at Robby and Robby picked up the coin from beneath the table.

What the hell is he so happy about? Dooks suddenly felt very wary. Robby was clearly smiling to himself behind his duct tape gag, and Dooks really wanted to know why. And for some reason, Robby seemed to be in no hurry to make his own throw. The sonofabitch seemed to be intent on making them suffer a long wait.

But it affects him too, Dooks thought. He looked over at Hicks. Hicks had begun sweating again. Profusely now.

Dooks looked back at Robby and made an impatient gesture. He now wished he didn't have duct tape over his mouth so he could ask Robby what he found so amusing.

Robby shrugged and waved the coin at them. Then he pointed his knife at himself and shook his head. After which he pointed the knife at both Dooks and Hicks, made a slashing gesture across his throat with the knife, and nodded.

Oh, my God, Dooks finally understood. *That drunken fool is telling us that it's one of us who's about to die, not himself. If he casts heads, Hicks is dead, and if he casts tails . . .*

Now the full import of what they were doing struck Dooks. As the seconds stretched out into a false eternity, an intense feeling of dread covered him and then seemed to settle down in his bones. He looked once more at Hicks, and saw that the big man was staring coldly back at him. Then Hicks pointed his knife at Robby and gestured to him to "Get on with it!"

Robby flipped the coin. Dooks watched it traverse space in its limited arc, spin thrice, and then Robby's right hand smacked it down on his left hand and covered it.

Once again Robby took his sweet time with letting them see the result. But this time, Dooks got the impression that he wasn't doing so just to torture them with apprehension. There was a calculating look in Robby's eyes now, as if he was sizing them both up, like a hunter deciding how best to kill the prey he was stalking.

Dooks remembered that Robby had been in the marines. *He's probably thinking he'll need to get me before I can reach the door and get away. Get away? That's a joke. If I lose the coin toss, both of these desperate men will be on me like white on rice, before I even make it out of this armchair . . . Sorry, Harry, but this is as far as it goes . . .*

Robby revealed what he'd thrown. Heads.

Dooks blasted a sigh of relief from his nostrils, while at the same time being fully aware that Hicks was emitting a shrill sound like the whimper of a scared puppy.

Robby was already out of his seat and advancing on Hicks with his knife poised to strike.

When Dooks turned towards Hicks, Hicks was holding his own knife in front of him, and waving it at them like a totem to banish evil.

Shock and fear had drained the color from his face, and yet he had a look of determination in his eyes, that spoke of his desire to remain alive.

This is something we didn't think of, Dooks realized. *That whoever lost would then change his mind about dying and fight to stay alive.*

It wasn't much of a fight though. Faced with Hicks's resistance, Robby had paused to consider the situation, but then Hicks reached up and began peeling the strip of tape off his face. Possibly deciding that Robby presented the real threat to his survival, he was focused on keeping Robby at bay.

That was his mistake. Dooks, realizing that once Hicks got that strip of silver tape off of his lips, there was as much chance of him yelling for help as there was of him trying to negotiate with them, threw caution to the winds and leapt in.

He stabbed Hicks deep in the belly, withdrew the knife and stabbed again.

Hicks immediately left off trying to free his mouth. Body stiffening in pain, he fell back into his chair and grabbed his belly.

Dooks stepped away from Hicks. His knife hand was covered in blood, and as he watched the blood pour out of Hicks, who was staring in horror at Robby and himself, the enormity of what he'd done struck him.

Shit—I've just killed Hicks!

This wasn't a hundred percent true yet, but the fact of Hicks's death was already settled. Robby was already slitting Hicks's throat, while Hicks, in too much pain to resist the fatal assault, was staring at Robby with tears in his eyes.

But Robby didn't relent. Another brutal slash, and Hicks slumped back with blood spilling down the front of his wifebeater.

Robby nodded at the corpse, then stepped back and peeled the duct tape off his mouth.

Dooks, now really feeling the magnitude of what he'd done, gaped at the dead man. Hicks lay with his beefy arms dangling over the side of his armchair, his knife on the patch of rug beneath his right hand. The amount of spilled blood was incredible.

"You'll get over it," Robby said, slapping Dooks on the shoulder. "First kill's always the worst. Once that's out of the way, you realize people are just skin bags full of meat and bones. Puncture them too badly and the blood all leaks out. That's what the marines taught me anyway."

Robby's shirt was splattered with blood. So much so, that at first glance, one might question exactly who had just been stabbed to death.

Dooks nodded and removed his own gag too. Something struck him them. "Hey, Robby, you aren't really drunk, are you?"

Robby grinned and shook his head. "With my life on the line? Are you kidding? I haven't had a drop since noon; that's mostly ginger ale in my flask, mixed with five percent vodka. But I had to put on an act for Hicks. He's a big guy, and I figured I couldn't take him drunk, if he lost and decided he'd fight it out instead of laying down and dying meekly like the Devil's Coin Game requires."

Dooks nodded. "And me?"

Robby laughed. "If you'd lost, you'd be easy to kill. You've no fighting experience. But Hicks? The guy used to fight in bars and he was brutal. Weren't that he was sick, he'd be almost impossible for us to manage, even with our knives."

Dooks nodded again. He didn't like the fact that Robby had dismissed him as an easy victim, but admitted his friend had a point. He looked around, saw Brownie was staring at them enquiringly; the pleading look in Brownie's eyes was almost as intense as Hicks had had while dying. The dog had no idea what was yet to come, but the smell of Hicks's spilling blood had to be reminding him that he was desperately hungry.

"So what now?" Dooks asked.

"Time to feed the dog." Robby pointed his bloody knife at Dooks's chest, then jabbed his thumb at the dead man in the chair. "You get the honorable job of cutting out Hicks's heart and convincing Brownie to eat it."

"Hey, why me?" Dooks protested. Even though he'd known from the get-go what the ritual consisted of, still the thought of having to butcher Hicks like that made him feel sick. Just killing the man had been bad enough.

Robby however laughed. "Why *you*? 'Cos it's time I had a drink, that's friggin' why. Being sober for so damn long is proving bad for my health. I'm starting to have withdrawal symptoms;"

After placing his knife on the coffee table and wiping his hands clean on a throw pillow, Robby flopped down on the couch, where he now pulled out another, previously unnoticed flask from his jacket. This one he uncapped and then took a long, long pull of his whiskey.

He snapped his fingers at Brownie. "Here, boy!" The dog joined him on the couch and had a nip of whiskey too, which seemed to deflect his hunger for the moment. Brownie was however still agitated by the smell of blood in the room and watched the corpse in interest as he sat by his owner.

Dooks sighed and then trudged over to Hicks. In transit to the corpse he paused to stare at the devil's coin on the coffee table. The coin lay on top of the Necromantica spellbook, which was now shut. It lay face up and the devil's face almost seemed to be mocking him.

With a deep shudder Dooks tore his gaze away from it. He stared at Hicks, stared at his knife, and then dug the blade into the dead man's belly.

Cutting Hicks's heart out of his body was slow and disgusting work. Dooks had never had an experience like this before and hoped never to have another. In two minutes both of his arms and his shirt were coated with gore and strange body fluids, and he realized that after they were done here, he and Robby would each need to borrow one of Hicks's oversize shirts to leave the Sunflower Motel without arousing suspicion.

Although Dooks knew that the human heart was situated on the left side of the body, he still had a lot of trouble reaching it. For one thing he had to cut his way through Hicks's lungs to reach the organ, and secondly, when he finally did get to the heart, it seemed more firmly rooted in place than a pillar stuck in cement. So he began slicing and hacking the fat-covered muscular pump free of its moorings.

Robby, meanwhile, concentrated on his drinking, occasionally offering dubiously helpful advice like, "Peel the belly skin off," "Hey, cut more to the left, not the friggin' right," and "Yeah, dude, just like that."

Ever since Dooks had begun cutting Hicks up, Robby had been restraining Brownie from crossing the room to investigate with a firm grip on the dog's leash.

Dooks ignored Robby and the dog and finally pulled Hicks's heart out of his body in more or less one piece. By now he was sweating, but his revulsion about the disgusting process of cutting Hicks open had faded.

I guess ends do justify means.

He held Hicks's heart towards Robby like an offering. "Hey, you fucking drunkard, where do we put the heart . . . and the dog?"

Robby thought for a moment, then got up from the couch: "I guess there's no point moving Brownie again. . . . And Hicks won't mind if we mess up his couch."

So, Dooks carried the heart over to the couch and dropped it down in front of the dog.

Brownie lurched at the heart the moment it was placed in front of him. But next he began whining and pawing furiously at the couch. The reason for this was because Robby was preventing him from reaching the heart.

"Hold on a damn minute, dog! It's all yours, but we've gotta read a spell while you eat it."

Robby nodded towards the table and Dooks picked up the spellbook. Neither of them were worried about staining the book red. Just like its cover, its pages also seemed made of skin. In any case, they didn't absorb water (a fact proved by the many times Robby had poured beer on them while studying the ritual), and also wiped clean easily (also proved when an inebriated Robby had puked on the pages during his magical studies).

Robby was seemingly exerting all of his strength to prevent Brownie consuming Hicks's heart, so it was up to Dooks to reopen the Necromantica to the relevant pages. Once he'd found the spell, he passed the book across to Robby, who then set the dog free to pounce on the heart.

Once free of his restraint, Brownie bit into Hicks's heart with such gusto that Dooks worried that he'd finish eating the organ before Robby even began reading the spell.

But once the dog's initial hunger pangs were satisfied, he took his time with eating the rest of the heart and Robby was soon deep into the spell:

"Manface nomed eht nommus ew won d'na . . ."

The spellbook said that once this spell was recited while the dog ate the loser's heart, the demon *Manface* would appear to grant their wishes.

However, the text didn't explain *how* the demon would appear to them, and so, as the spell proceeded and Brownie continued to satisfy his hunger on the fast-shrinking organ that had once belonged to the dead man across the room, Dooks again felt a sense of dread.

CHAPTER 4

Roman

In Room 7 of the front block of the Sunflower Motel, Roman Fowler's emotions were a bittersweet cocktail. On the one hand he'd just successfully inked a new deal for his bosses (he worked for a company that sold lighting fixtures). On the other hand, the escort he'd hired to celebrate his success had called him a short while ago to say she couldn't make it anymore. Something she'd had for lunch had disagreed with her . . .

She'd asked if she could send a friend over in her place, but Roman had told her not to mind; he'd call her the next time he was in Raynham. He'd considering taking on the replacement prostitute, but he had no idea what she'd look like, and this girl he'd initially ordered looked like an ex-girlfriend of his did—she had the same slim face, same long black hair, and the same kind of figure—so in that sense she'd have been a nostalgia fuck.

Since then Roman had been drinking. He'd already gotten a good buzz on and was watching TV. But he now felt uncomfortable. A short while ago while surfing channels he'd made the mistake of watching ten minutes or so of a softcore movie, and this had given him an erection, a stiffening of the penis which was refusing to deflate no matter how much beer he drank or how much he thought of that horrid piece of roadkill he'd noticed roadside on his drive back up from Taunton—the dead creature had been quite big, and so smashed and squirted inside-out that it was impossible to tell what it had been: porcupine, raccoon, fawn, bear cub, or someone's unfortunate dog or cat.

But even concentrating hard on that revolting mess of intestines and brain matter and ugh! . . . didn't help any. Just when Roman thought he'd gotten a little penile deflation going, the image of the giant breasts in that softcore movie reared up in his mind again and Roman's penis reared up also and resumed its sentinel duty in his shorts. Each time he looked down at his crotch, he saw the round fat head of his cock poking out of his shorts like someone looking out of a tent; tempting him to switch channels from the sports interview he'd finally chosen to watch and return the TV to the channel with the gorgeous actresses and masturbate.

Roman, however, wasn't in any mood to jerk off; after turning down that offer of a replacement prostitute, masturbation seemed a very poor substitute. Besides, he didn't feel any sexual desperation. The beer was settling in nicely, he felt lazy and relaxed, the TV interview was engrossing, and other than for his erection all was right with his world.

A commercial break came on. Roman considered popping into the bathroom for a quick cold shower.

And then someone knocked on the door. Once, twice . . . three times, then silence.

Roman put his beer down on the end table near his chair and got to his feet.

The knock came again. Soft but rapid, like the person was in a hurry . . . or in danger even.

"Yeah, hold on, I'm coming," Roman said, lumbering to his feet. He was halfway to the door before he remembered his erection. He looked down at his shorts, was tipsy enough to think his dangling shirt would conceal his penile discomfort from whoever was knocking, and shambled over the front door.

The security chain was off because he'd been expecting someone and so he simply pulled the door open.

But there was no one out there. Roman stood at the threshold with wind blowing in his face, looking left and right for who'd knocked. Opposite him stood the wall of trees that separated the motel from Carver Street, their leaves agitated by the same wind that was rustling his brown hair. The wind carried a hint of rain to come, or maybe it was already falling somewhere nearby.

Except for Roman's car and a few others, the parking lot was a bare concrete expanse.

"That can't be just an echo from the TV that I just heard," he said aloud in some confusion, turning and looking back at the unit. "And both rooms either side of me don't seem occupied."

It occurred to Roman that whoever had knocked might be hiding behind his car. That alarmed him slightly; that he might be attacked.

But still, maybe because he'd been drinking, he felt the need to investigate that possibility. His blue Nissan SUV was on his left and he stepped towards it.

But before he reached the SUV, he heard the rush of frantic footsteps heading towards him.

He spun around and saw a woman heading for him, hurrying over from the direction of the reception building. She wasn't running, just walking very fast; her high heels clopping noisily on the walkway corridor. He felt some relief on seeing she wasn't armed.

As she got closer, Roman recognized her; or rather he recognized her clingy blue dress. He'd seen her earlier tonight, when he'd arrived back here from Taunton. She had been standing at the turnoff into the motel driveway. The way her breasts were struggling their way out of her dress with no attempt on her part to restrain them again, he'd instantly pegged her as a hooker.

There had been something strange about his noticing her back then. One minute she'd been standing there on the sidewalk, giving him the eye, and a moment later, after he'd glanced into his offside mirror, she wasn't there anymore, like she'd sprinted away silently to hide amongst the trees. He'd looked around for her dark hair and blue dress and it was almost like she'd never existed.

In passing, the experience had been a little spooky. But Roman had been expecting the escort he'd hired and so hadn't given the matter much thought.

Now she reached him and stopped.

Once more something about this prostitute immediately struck Roman as abnormal; though other than the amount of makeup she was wearing, he couldn't have said what it was. So yes, maybe it was just her makeup. She was wearing so much foundation, eyeliner, mascara, blush, and lipstick that Roman couldn't tell how old she was. But she nonetheless had a wasted look in her eyes that spoke of a person who'd gone too far too fast. Regardless of her age, as a prostitute this woman was on the decline, and it was down a fast and brutal slope at that.

She was staring at him, but not at his face. It took Roman a moment to realize that she was looking at his penis, which was still erect and lifting up the right lower hem of his shorts. Maybe it had previously been deflating, but this woman's arrival had revived it.

"Hey, you need some help with that?" she asked, reaching out to touch his protruding penis. "Looks like you do, honey."

Roman evaded her questing fingers just in time. Though still mortified that she'd noticed, her being a prostitute canceled out the incident's embarrassment. She seemed completely unflustered by his rampant state; so why should he be?

She probably even approves of it, as it makes me a potential customer.

"Are you the one who just knocked on my door?" he asked as she stared at him.

However, he didn't see how she could be the person who'd knocked. After doing so, she would have had no time to get back to where he'd noticed her approaching from. He'd definitely not heard her high heels departing from his door. And, considering that the first time he'd looked that way, there had been no one there (he knew he'd not drank enough yet to give himself minus-vision), she could only have come from around the side of the building, which was about fifty yards off. Either that or she'd come out of one of the other motel rooms along the block. But the two rooms that way which appeared occupied were both nearer to him than where he'd seen her coming from.

There was one other option, but he quickly dismissed it. The front block was built with a space between Rooms 5 and 6—a wide passageway that led to the rear of the motel—and so she could have ducked through there, but . . . but she had come from further away than there. To Roman's mind, there was no way that she could have ducked into the passageway, run around the end of the block and reached where he'd noticed her in the short interval since she'd knocked the door and he'd opened it. In addition to the fact that it would be an utterly silly thing to do except she was high on drugs, there was the sheer physical impossibility of the feat to consider, considering the fact that she was wearing high heels.

So, is she the one who knocked on my door, or was I hearing things?

"Yeah, that was me," the woman quickly replied, thankfully seeming to forget his sexually aroused state, then she gestured towards his open motel room. "Hey, I'm real sorry to bother you like this, but can I use your bathroom?"

Bemused, he nodded and she rushed past him and into his room. He turned around slowly, and, still wondering how she'd managed what she claimed to have done, walked in after her.

As Roman shut the motel room door behind them, he began willing his stubborn erection to go down before she got out of his bathroom.

CHAPTER 5

Mandy Cherry & Dewdrop

"Hey, baby, something just came to my mind," Dewdrop said as Mandy slowly maneuvered their car into parking near Room 13. "Not saying it's anything serious, like, but . . . you know . . ."

"What's on your mind?" Mandy asked and switched off the engine.

Room 13's lights were on. Since Tenebra was expecting them, she would surely have heard their car stop. That was, unless she'd fallen asleep watching TV; low-level ambient noise came from the room and screen flicker played against her shut drapes. Room 13 was the third room on this block; they'd had to drive almost the whole way back between the front and middle blocks to reach it. Tenebra's right-hand neighbor had their lights on too, but the two rooms to the left of hers—14 and 15—both had their lights off. The distribution of vehicles along the middle block mostly matched the window illumination.

Tenebra's lime-green Kia sedan faced her room. After some consideration Mandy had decided against parking beside it, facing Room 14, but had instead parked the Honda along the axis of the motel buildings, so they didn't need to reverse the car before leaving, but could simply speed off once the bloody deed was completed.

Mandy had also been careful to park in what she considered a dead spot outside of the range of the single CCTV camera that monitored the comings and goings along the middle block's external corridor.

"I dunno if it's 'cos of that hooker we just ran into, or because she's rooming in Room 13," Dewdrop explained, giggling a little nervously, but I've just been remembering what Petra said was her reason for breaking up with Tenebra."

Mandy felt an unwelcome shiver in her chest. "About Tenebra being a witch?"

Dewdrop shrugged and locked fingers with Mandy across the gearshift. Mandy felt her girlfriend's body tingling with excitement; or was it fright?

"Yeah, that," Dewdrop agreed. "Okay, so maybe Petra didn't exactly call her a witch, but she hinted as much. She said Tenebra was into the occult in a big way, and she'd slowly grown more and more frightened of her."

Mandy laughed. "Yeah, frightened enough to kill her."

"Whatever. But she meant it. I remember the fear in her eyes."

Mandy opened up the glove compartment and from it removed two black baseball caps, two pairs of dark sunglasses, and two pairs of black gloves. She handed one set of cap, gloves and sunglasses to Dewdrop and put the others on herself. Now looking like the career criminal she was, she smiled grimly at Dewdrop.

"Get out of the car before you start me seeing spooks," she instructed Dewdrop, and pushed her own door open. She gestured to the backseat with her thumb. "And don't forget your toolbox."

'Toolbox' slung over her shoulder, Dewdrop shortly joined Mandy outside the car. They stood by the driver's door and stared the ten yards across to Room 13. Tenebra's car blocked their vision of the door, but they made out a face peering through parted drapes at the window.

"I've also been thinking about that witchcraft story," Mandy admitted in a low whisper. "But even if it's true, it won't stop Tenebra bleeding to death when we stab her." Mandy spoke like this to bolster her courage. Now that Dewdrop had opened this can of worms, she felt a return of her earlier dread after they'd encountered the hooker at the edge of the front block, which now stood behind them like a giant mausoleum, occasionally punctuating the thrumming night noises of nature with bursts of human conversation and television chatter and music.

"You know, maybe you were right," Dewdrop said nervously.

"Right about what?"

"About what you said earlier. You know, how you felt like tonight wasn't the best night for killing Tenebra." She gestured languidly out over the end of the middle block's rooftop, where the moon glowed like candlelight over the trees. "We could drive off now . . . give Petra an excuse . . . come back tomorrow." She giggled. "My pussy's hungry for yours—let's go scissor."

Mandy rolled her eyes. "We'll scissor on Tenebra's corpse." She nudged Dewdrop hard with her elbow. "Pull your mind out of the gutter and focus."

"Was just a suggestion," Dewdrop said, her voice wistful.

"You're forgetting that Tenebra's already seen us," Mandy pointed out, adjusting the baseball cap on her head. "We drive off now, and she's gonna call Petra and rail at her. What explanation would we give for just driving off?"

"Um, maybe that we forgot her money?"

Mandy thought about it. Her own fear was returning, but she saw no reason why it should do so . . . until she remembered the photo of Tenebra that Petra had sent to both of their cellphones. Yes, Tenebra (real name Amy Grace Watkins) was a very attractive woman; she had long black hair, striking eyes and perfect lips and nose; one could easily see what a rich socialite like Petra Velli had seen in her. But there had been something wrong about her face. Her smiling lips had suggested not just wantonness, but also . . . sadism.

Remembering that face now, Mandy understood what the problem was. In that photograph, Tenebra had looked like she really liked hurting people; in her face there had been more than a hint of nastiness, dark deviant script written behind bright blue eyes, maybe even coded into her retinal patterns. Mandy figured that if she and Dewdrop had bothered to ask Mrs. Velli for more details of her ex's deviation from socially acceptable behavior, tales of intense sadomasochism would certainly have followed.

Still, Mandy decided there was no point putting off their hit, just because they were getting the heebie-jeebies. The supernatural might be scary, but she'd so far had no experience with it; neither had Dewdrop, as far as she knew. But they both had experience with sadists; both with fucking them, and with killing them.

"What do you think?" Dewdrop was asking, her voice very nervous now. "We really could say we forgot to bring the money along? Or, hey—we could say we forgot that amulet thingy she wants! Tenebra can't argue that excuse; she was insistent that without the amulet there's no deal. We'll tell Petra the same . . . or lie that we heard the cops drive past."

The amulet. Mandy Cherry had forgotten about Tenebra's amulet. She'd given it to Petra when they were still in lust with each other. And now she'd insisted she wanted it back; along with her two hundred grand blackmail payment. The amulet was in Dewdrop's pocket. Mandy thought it was creepy, but Dewdrop thought it was cute.

"Forget it," Mandy whispered harshly, feeling a revival of her courage. "And I don't mean we forget the hit. Let's do the job we came here for. We'll take care of Tenebra first and then we'll take that hooker away from here with us and kill her too."

"Okay, you're the lady boss," Dewdrop quickly agreed. She perked up so quickly that Mandy realized her girlfriend had just been toying with her, trying to see how far her courage would stretch. She flexed her fist. *Later, you horny bitch, I'll stretch you till you beg for mercy.*

"Well, are you coming or not?" Dewdrop asked, stepping forward past the trunk of the green car. "Let's kill Tenebra."

***

The door to Room 13 opened on the second knock. The door was on the chain, and Tenebra's face appeared in the slight gap. For some reason, just like the hooker they planned on killing after they'd killed her, Tenebra was also wearing a lot of makeup. Her lips were painted so black, her mouth looked like a mine shaft. And she had on a mixture of black and red eyeshadow. Total witch, but Mandy refused to be spooked, which she supposed was the idea behind the makeup.

Like she'd been about going to bed, Tenebra had on a black nightgown.

"Hey, fucking let us in. You know who we are and why we're here," Mandy grunted.

"Do you have my necklace?" Tenebra asked.

Mandy didn't get why the woman considered the amulet so important. *Soon you'll be dead and have no need for it.* "Yeah, we brought it with us."

"Where is it then? Lemme see it. I'm not letting you girls in here, except you've got the amulet with you."

"Here it is, lady." Dewdrop dangled the amulet before Tenebra's eyes.

Mandy hid her revulsion. The amulet was designed like a very ugly demon's head, complete with horns and evil leer. "Now that you know we brought it with us," she said, "will you fucking take the chain off of the goddamn door and let us inside? Someone is soon gonna wonder what we're doing out here." Then a thought occurred to her. "Or is there someone in there with you? Your boyfriend?"

"If there is, that won't work," Dewdrop said. "We'll be leaving, 'cos we don't want any witnesses to this."

"Or anyone jumping us, for that matter," Mandy improvised.

Tenebra shook her head quickly. "No, I'm all alone. Yeah, I guess you girls had better come in."

Mandy counted seconds while Tenebra pushed the door almost shut again, slid back the chain latch, and then reopened it.

***

Tenebra was older than she'd appeared in her photograph, in which she had seemed to be about the same age as Mandy and Dewdrop. And in addition, met in person, her face lacked the sadism Mandy had earlier noticed in it; which meant she'd just been looking mean for the camera. Mandy felt relieved by this. This woman wouldn't be any trouble to deal with. She felt surprised that Tenebra had even worked up the courage to blackmail Petra Velli.

I guess the amulet really does mean a lot to her. Either that or she's got gambling markers to cover.

Mandy quickly deduced that Tenebra either wasn't a very experienced blackmailer or she wasn't a very smart person. No sooner had she let them into the room and shut the door, than she turned her back on them and looked at the TV instead, which was showing a 40's black-and-white sci-fi flick complete with men-in-latex-suit aliens and gorgeous busty women who needed saving from them.

There were two wineglasses on the coffee table, along with a half empty bottle of Chianti; and this made Mandy realize that although Tenebra did not currently have company, she must have had some earlier.

Whatever else may have struck her as odd about this scenario she ignored, putting it down to her initial worries about Tenebra being a witch.

"Have a seat, both of you," Tenebra was saying. "Would you like some wi—?"

She never finished the statement. On a signal from Mandy, she and Dewdrop jumped Tenebra.

This was a maneuver they had practiced and executed many times before, and it came out perfectly now, with Mandy clamping a napkin over Tenebra's mouth from behind while Dewdrop shoved her down onto the couch.

"Quick, check the bathroom, make sure no one's there!" Dewdrop said throatily. She held Tenebra in place on the couch with a knife pressed to her throat.

Mandy quickly looked into the bathroom. "It's empty," she told Dewdrop, pulling off her shades and baseball cap and dropping them on the bed. Then she walked back over to the scared woman on the couch.

Tenebra was trying to protest to them, but Dewdrop had stuffed the napkin deep into her mouth and her complaints came out muffled. Both girls weren't interested in what she had to say anyway. Mandy was delighted that this was proceeding smoothly.

"You do her while I film it," she told Dewdrop.

Mandy got out her cellphone and began filming.

"Okay," Dewdrop said, pressing her knife against Tenebra's neck. "This is the part where you come to the sad and pathetic realization that blackmail don't pay. Particularly not when you put the screws to a rich bitch like Petra Velli. And now, Tenebra, on behalf of Mrs. Velli, we're gonna crush ya like a bug being squashed under her designer high heels. 'Cos in reality, that's all you are."

Tenebra was gaping wide-eyed now. "Hmmph! Hmmph!" But she had no reprieve. Despite the threat of the knife at her throat, she tried to get away, but as she leapt up, Dewdrop stabbed her deep in the belly.

All the fight instantly left Tenebra. She sank back down on the couch.

"Where d'you think you're going?" Mandy asked, stepping close up to record the red stream coming from Tenebra's belly, as Dewdrop twisted the knife about in her punctured flesh. Her blood quickly soaked through her nightgown. Dewdrop pulled out the knife and stabbed Tenebra again. Once more she twisted the knife, to both cause maximum pain and do the maximum damage to her victim's body. She was grinning, her teeth bright ivory in her flushed face.

Tenebra began flopping about on the couch, her arms flailing, her legs kicking as she expired.

"Get out of the shot," Mandy grunted, so Dewdrop got out of her way and let her film Tenebra's nasty death.

It was over in a few seconds more. Tenebra went completely limp, her brown eyes open, glassy as marbles and seeing nothing.

Dewdrop walked over to her leather 'toolbox.' "Okay, time for the money shot," she announced.

Mandy nodded. Dewdrop pulled out a meat cleaver and began hacking off Tenebra's head against the edge of the coffee table. She did so violently—thump, thump, thump—it sounded like someone chopping beef. Mandy moved in close for better camera focus. Dewdrop was proving she'd had previous experience with performing a decapitation; she was getting very little blood on her clothes.

Finally, Tenebra's head separated from her body. Dewdrop shoved the headless body back onto the couch, and stood up dangling the head by its hair. She was breathing heavily, her breasts rising and falling both from exertion and her excitement.

"Well, that's this month's rent paid," she said, while raising Tenebra's head for Mandy to get a good close-up of it.

"Okay, we're good," Mandy said, lowering the cellphone. "I've sent the video to Mrs. Velli. Our balance payment should shortly hit my account." She giggled. "That of course, is after she gets through vomiting. I'm certain she's squeamish."

"Petra Velli certainly won't have any complaints about the show we just put on," Dewdrop said, then she turned Tenebra's face towards her and began making faces at it. "You're a great snuff movie actress, Tenebra," she told the gaping, staring head, then pulled the napkin out of its mouth so its mouth was also gaping at her.

Mandy nodded. "Oh, Mrs. Velli will be pleased as punch." Staring at the dead woman made her feel very good. She always felt great after killing someone. It wasn't a sexual feeling like Dewdrop got, just the result of a subconscious appreciation of the fact that she was still alive.

However, it was time to leave. Time to go soak in a hot bubble bath for a while and then, maybe . . .

She winked at Dewdrop. "Hey, baby, drop the head and let's go."

But Dewdrop was staring in bemusement at the dead head she was holding. "Okay, now this is weird. This is really weird."

Mandy at first thought her girlfriend was messing with her again, like she'd done before they had entered the room. "Look, Dewy, just drop the damn head and let's get the hell out of here. She's dead, she can't give you head, but I can, and if you keep fucking with me tonight you won't be getting any."

But no, Dewdrop was staring at her with a partly amused and partly worried look on her face. "Mandy, I think we just hit the wrong woman."

Mandy froze. *What?* She felt like her blood had turned to ice in her veins. "What?"

Dewdrop nodded vigorously. "Yeah, yeah." She gestured with her chin at Mandy's cellphone. "Look, open up the picture of Tenebra that Petra sent us. My hand are too bloody to use my cellphone."

Mandy quickly opened up Telegram and located the image Dewdrop wanted.

"Here it is," she said.

"Expand her head a bit. Lemme see her ears."

Mandy still thought Dewdrop was mistaken, but she did so.

Dewdrop studied the picture for all of five seconds then looked up with a grim expression on her face. "No doubt about it, this isn't Tenebra Watkins."

Mandy studied the picture and then the severed head her girlfriend was holding. "What makes you say that? The only difference I can see is that it's an old photo of hers, maybe from seven or eight years ago."

"The number of ear piercings are different," Dewdrop explained. "The Tenebra in this picture has three piercings in her left ear. This dead bitch"—she turned the head so Mandy could see what she meant—"has just one." She sighed. "And also—though I don't know how in hell we could have missed it, except we're getting really sloppy—in the photo Tenebra has blue eyes . . . this woman's eyes are brown."

"Contact lenses," Mandy immediately replied, still unwilling to believe they'd made such a big error. "I sort of noticed her eyes when we arrived, but I didn't consider it a big deal. People wear fashionable contacts all the time. And remember she was dating Petra, who's very high-class."

"Okay, yes," Dewdrop agreed patiently, while studying the severed head for answers. "Contact lenses would explain the difference in eye color, but not how she suddenly has less ear piercings than before. It would make sense if she now had *more* piercings, but not *less*."

Mandy was forced to accept the truth. She even found some humor in their situation. *And I've just uploaded the file of this bitch's death to our client?* She was now well past her initial shock at the discovery of their error. Their having killed the wrong person didn't bother her in the least.

"So, if this woman ain't Tenebra," Dewdrop asked. "Where is she?"

"Good question," Mandy agreed. Then she pointed to the pair of wineglasses and the half-empty bottle of Chianti on the coffee table. "I'd say that's a clue. It means Tenebra was here earlier. But then, where did she go?"

"Maybe she stepped outside for a bit, went to buy something."

Mandy shook her head. "That can't be right; her car is parked outside."

Dewdrop finally dropped the dead woman's head on the couch beside her body. "Not necessarily," she pointed out. "The green car might belong to this bitch we killed. Maybe they're partners in the blackmail scheme."

Mandy accepted that. "Yeah. That would also explain how this woman knew we had the amulet with us. Gimme the amulet."

Her mind was whirling with thoughts. Where the hell was Tenebra?

She waited till Dewdrop had handed the amulet to her, then said, "I'm thinking that you're right. Maybe all we need to do is wait. If Tenebra rushed out to buy tampons or something she'll be back soon."

Mandy was distracted by the amulet. She'd just recalled how much she disliked looking at it and wondered why she'd even just requested that Dewdrop hand it over. Spur of the moment, of course.

"You know, we could just call her," Dewdrop said.

"Huh?"

Dewdrop shrugged. "Yeah, girl, call Tenebra on your phone. Tell her we're here with her money and her amulet and her friend, and ask her where exactly she is. She won't be expecting us to jump her once she gets back here."

Mandy nodded and kissed Dewdrop. "Honey, sometimes you're so smart you win my heart all over again."

She stuffed the amulet away in a pocket, opened up the call log in her cellphone, and dialed Tenebra.

But even before the phone began ringing, Mandy realized that something was wrong. She and Dewdrop had overlooked something important.

We're overconfident . . . no, no, no—Tenebra was expecting us . . . she left this woman who looks exactly like herself here as a decoy to throw us off . . .

But Tenebra's phone had begun ringing; right there in the motel room with them.

Mandy at first wondered where exactly the ringing sound was coming from. It was behind her, and she turned to locate it. It seemed that Tenebra had left her phone in the motel room. But there was no cellphone in sight.

In the meantime Dewdrop had sauntered around to the television, which was now showing the end credits for the 40's sci-fi flick. She too looked around for the ringing phone.

And that was when Mandy saw the shadows in the corner behind Dewdrop come alive.

The shadows seemed to become liquid, like in a film CGI transformation scene. The liquid form reflected light in a swirling tapestry of colors. This shimmering effect had a hypnotic effect on Mandy and she stood entranced, watching the hardening and lightening darkness resolve itself into the shape of a woman. A woman with long black hair and who was holding a long black knife.

Tenebra. The real one. The cruel look in her eyes was unmistakable. And yet the swirling playground of color as Tenebra became solid was so entrancing, so lulling, that Mandy found it impossible to call out a warning to her girlfriend.

Dewdrop noticed the dreamy look on Mandy's face. "Why do you look stunned all of a sudden?" she asked.

"Be-be-behind you! Look out!" Mandy said, coming out of her freeze. But she'd delayed too long before giving the warning.

Alarmed by her girlfriend's alarm, Dewdrop began turning. But the woman behind her took two steps forward and stabbed the knife into her back.

Mandy watched helplessly. Tenebra had struck upward into Mandy's body from about the height of her kidneys. She had clearly aimed for Dewdrop's heart and the look on Dewdrop's face—the way she gasped in agony as the knife hit the bullseye—shattered Mandy's cold heart. With a strength that seemed supernatural, Tenebra rammed the knife further into Dewdrop's body until the tip of its reddened black blade emerged from Dewdrop's chest, puncturing her left breast and jutting out like a steel nipple that dispensed blood instead of milk.

43

Dewdrop sank to the floor, gasping for breath and choking on her own blood. As she fell her weight yanked the hilt of the knife out of Tenebra's hand. Down on the floor, Dewdrop reached out a hand to Mandy for help, gaped at her in confusion, and died.

Mandy stared at Dewdrop for a while, trying to come to terms with what had just happened. She was about looking up at Tenebra's face, but then found she had no need to do so, because Tenebra bent down over Dewdrop and began pulling the knife out of her back.

Tenebra frowned up at Mandy. Her blue eyes were impossibly evil in her beautiful face.

"I was almost hoping you two degenerates would decide I was dead and ride off to your happily-ever-after ending," she told Mandy. "Then I wouldn't have to kill you both." She scowled. "But I guess it's like they say—what will be will be. White mice never learn their lesson about messing with black cats."

Mandy's courage melted. In any normal state of affairs, she would have taken Tenebra on. Even though the knife the other woman had just slid out of Dewdrop's body was about a foot long, Mandy was both brave enough and experienced enough in knife fighting to deflect the blade face-to-face and hand Tenebra's ass to her on a plate.

But her bravery was negated by what she'd seen. This woman had just appeared out of nothingness, had solidified out of shadow. That was inexplicable, and if Mandy wasn't scared of Tenebra herself, she was understandably terrified of the powers she commanded.

So Mandy did the one thing that made sense in this situation. She turned and dashed for the door. She knew she'd easily make it outside. There were three yards of space between Tenebra and herself. Also, before Tenebra could reach her, she would both need to straighten up to her feet and also navigate her way around both Dewdrop's corpse and the coffee table.

But that wasn't how things played out.

Mandy reached the door and worked the handle, while behind her Tenebra uttered a guttural command:

"Reh, pots d'na nekawa, namow daed!"

Mandy was shocked when the door ceased opening. Thinking Tenebra had cast a spell on it, she panicked and tried to force it to move.

Open up, damn you!

Through the crack of door, she could see her car and the safety of the night. She didn't look back at Tenebra, whom she was certain was right behind her now, preparing to strike her too in the back like she'd done to Dewdrop.

But then she realized that the reason the door wasn't opening was because, not wanting to be disturbed during their grisly business earlier, Dewdrop had put the chain back on it after they'd stepped into the room.

Shit! Mandy thought, now closing the door and working on the chain.

She got the chain off quickly, but before she could get the door open again and run out into safety, a hand grabbed her ankle. Mandy looked down at her foot and her mind seemed to puree in disbelief.

The dead woman—the *headless* dead woman—had her by the heel. Her body lying on the floor, the fingers of the corpse's left hand were clamped around Mandy's left ankle. And while Mandy gaped and tried to kick free, the headless body pulled itself forward and grabbed hold of Mandy's right ankle too with its right hand. The corpse's grip felt like iron manacles.

Mandy stopped gaping at the reanimated corpse gripping her legs and gaped at Tenebra instead. "Wha-wha-wha . . . ?"

Tenebra hadn't moved from where she was. She was still beside the TV, standing now, and with her black knife back in her hand and dripping Dewdrop's blood on the rug.

"Tuo reh k'conk!" Tenebra said, again in that guttural language Mandy had never heard spoken anywhere else.

Mandy was still gaping in confusion when the corpse gave both of her legs a violent upward yank that flung her through the air, so that she crashed against the door.

What just happened in here? Mandy thought, right before her head smacked into the door handle and she was knocked unconscious.

CHAPTER 6

Dooks, Robby & . . . ?

". . . Su ot raeppa, Manface!" Robby concluded the spell and fell silent.

As far as Dooks could tell, Robby had rushed through the spell to get it completed before Brownie finished eating Hicks's heart. He'd finished with maybe a bite or two of heart meat left to spare.

However, it looked like it might still be a while before those two bites of heart found their way down the dog's digestive tract. Brownie was chewing contentedly, in no rush now that his initial pangs of hunger had been assuaged. As Dooks waited, a strange inertia settled over him.

The manual—that God-damned spellbook—says that once the dog eats the heart, the demon 'Manface' will appear and grant us our wishes.

"I wish we could hurry the mutt up," he told Robby.

Robby set the spellbook down on the table. "Dude, there's no rush. We still got all night." Then he grimaced. Robby's body really didn't work too good anymore. Those three bullets he'd taken in Iraq had messed him up. The doctors had patched him up as best they could, but, even with the painkillers he was on, lots of times he was in severe pain and even when he wasn't, his right leg twitched a lot, like it was doing now.

Robby grabbed his belly and froze, a stray muscle twitching in his left cheek. Then he reached for the silvery flask of booze and took a long swig. After three or four seconds, he removed the flask from his lips and looked at it in disgust. Then he dropped it on the floor and strained to his feet. "Hicks is certain to have some good whiskey somewhere in this dump."

Before starting his search, Robbie gently patted Brownie on the head and pointed to the small uneaten part of the heart. "Hey, boy, hurry up with that. Don't worry, Brownie, after tonight we'll be rich, and then no more leftover burgers for ya!"

Robby stalked off towards the nook that had served Hicks as a kitchenette. He walked with one hand pressed to his belly like he'd just gotten gut-shot all over again.

This poor sonofabitch needs to wish for good health, not the hundred million bucks he intends to, Dooks thought in a burst of sympathy as Robby began opening the shelves over the kitchenette sink. And as for me, *I'm not shortchanging myself like Robby is doing. I'm wishing for a cool billion bucks!*

Feeling a sudden pang of guilt about the source of their wealth, Dooks glanced over at Hicks's body. The big guy was a gruesome sight, sprawled there in the chair like he'd had a heart attack while bathing with catsup.

Worst of all, Hicks was staring right at Dooks. At least he seemed to be doing so.

Dooks got to his feet and walked over to Hicks. He closed the corpse's eyes. Doing so immediately made him feel better; at least until he made the mistake of glancing down at the mess he'd made of Hicks belly while extracting his heart.

Feeling like he'd throw up, Dooks turned away, just in time to see Robby emerge from the kitchenette with a 'eureka' look on his face and two bottles of Wild Turkey 101 bourbon in his hands.

"Dog finished eating the heart yet?" Robby asked nonchalantly.

"Just about," Dooks replied, while wondering how Robby could seem so unconcerned. *Me, I'm so nervous, that . . . that . . .*

"Hey, do you intend on drinking all that whiskey tonight?" he asked Robby to calm his own nerves.

Robby nodded. "Maybe. Depends on how long this stuff takes to get done with." With a bottle, he gestured to the spellbook. "We've performed the ritual, now we've just gotta wait for that demon Manface to turn up like the genie in the lamp."

Robbie put down the bottles of liquor on the coffee table and picked up the TV remote control instead. "And personally, I can't think of a better way to pass the time than drinkin' and watching TV. Gonna find me a horror flick full of tits and ass to watch. Who the hell knows how long it's gonna take for Manface to show up."

"Y-Y-You know, I-I-I-I don't think it's g-g-gonna t-t-take all th-th-that long," Dooks stuttered in a trembling voice. "Br-br-brownie . . . Brownie . . ."

Robby had been aiming the remote at the TV, but now he turned to look at Brownie.

"Shit!" he exclaimed, the remote control dropping from his hand. "The book don't say anything about this happening!" He glanced for a moment at the Necromantica spellbook and then back at his dog.

Brownie was altering. From his normal furry brown form, the dog was turning coal-black. In addition his body was becoming rigid.

Sensing that something was wrong with him, Brownie tried getting down from the couch and going over to his owner for assistance, but instead he became frozen on the edge of the couch, with his forepaws dangling out in midair.

The dog visibly became rigid as a statue, but that wasn't the worst of it. The moment after he completely froze into immobility, Brownie's head altered, with his face becoming that of Hicks. What now faced the two men was a mad melding of human face and dog body of carved rock.

"Shit, so that's what the name 'Manface' means," Dooks said. Then, realizing the implication of what had just happened to the dog, he and Robby both turned to stare at the dead man behind them.

"What the . . . ?" Dooks was so frightened he took several steps backward.

Hicks no longer had a face. The front of his head—everything ahead of his ears—was a featureless mass of smooth flesh. Dooks didn't know whether to be relieved or scared by this; a faceless skull like this sure beat the hell out of Hicks now having a dog's head on his shoulders.

Dooks looked at Robby; Robby stared back at him. Their confusion had little time to germinate however, as they were startled by another noise behind them, and were forced to turn and face the demon they had just summoned.

The demon was making a weird noise; like it was trying to speak to them, but couldn't.

Dooks realized what the problem was: Hicks's face still had the strip of duct tape over its mouth. Dooks hurriedly removed the strip of tape.

"Sorry 'bout that," he apologized, stepping back to what he considered a safe distance from the creature. Though its body seemed completely frozen in place like it was a modern-day sphinx, still Dooks saw no point in taking chances. He didn't like the look of this

'Manface' thing. Hicks's face now had an evil aspect to it that it hadn't previously possessed. Yes, the original Hicks had looked a little mean, but now . . . ?

Dooks couldn't really put into words what the demon's ownership of this human visage had infected it with, but it was very horrible indeed. If the original Hicks had been a common flu virus, this new Manface version of him was an epidemic.

"My name is Manface," the demon announced in a voice somewhere between a canine growl and Hicks's baritone rumble, "you have summoned me correctly for the Devil's Coin Game." It frowned. "And now, let us proceed with the ritual."

"Yes," Dooks agreed. "What I want to wish for is a whole lot of money—a billion dollars at least."

But if Dooks had expected the dog-demon to leap to supplying him with a yacht, a villa, and a billion dollars in the bank, he was sorely disappointed. What it instead said was: "The sole survivor's requests will be attended to when the ritual reaches its conclusion."

The demon's comment made Dooks stop cold. *Sole survivor . . . Conclusion . . . Oh, my God . . . Robby fucked up.*

His relief at their having successfully concluded the night's grisly business evaporated. Or maybe it drained out of him like piss under pressure.

He stared in horror at their transformed dog. "Mutt, what the fuck are you talking about?"

The dog-demon seemed to sigh. "There are two versions of the Devil's Coin Game, Harry Dooks," it replied. "In the basic version with three players, both survivors are granted a single wish. In the more advanced version of the game, however, there is only a single survivor, and this person receives two wishes to be granted." The demon paused for a moment as if trying to draw breath, and then finished, "Your companion and yourself performed the latter version of the ritual. Hence, you must continue to play till only one of you remains alive, and I will then grant two wishes to that person."

Stunned, Dooks turned to look at his friend. "Robby, I thought you said you hadn't been drinking. What the hell did you just go and do?"

Robby looked at him apologetically and shrugged like he was sorry at making a honest mistake. But all of a sudden Dooks wasn't buying that innocent act of his anymore. "Hey, you sack of shit, you did this intentionally, didn't you?"

Dooks had to give Robby credit; the sonofabitch kept up that innocent act for a full five seconds longer. Then he sighed and nodded. "Yeah, Harry, I did."

"But why, man? Why? We each already had a wish each. We'd both have been okay with that."

But even while speaking, Dooks already knew the answer. One wish wouldn't be enough for Robby. *All Robby's any good for at the moment is Jack shit, and Jack already left town.*

"I'm sorry, Harry, but one wish won't do me any good," Robby said by way of confirmation. You know what I was gonna wish for— to be free of this constant pain I'm in. But, see, that's the problem, isn't it? If I wish away the pain, then what's left for me? I'll still be a broke bum, reliant on the disability pension and a lifetime of handouts . . ."

"But I was gonna wish for a billion bucks! I'd gladly have given you some of it."

Robby laughed sardonically. "Yeah, I'm sure you would, Harry. You're a good friend. But for how long was I gonna be reliant on you?" Robby frowned and his eyes turned steely; the gaze he must have turned on the Iraqis and on his dead comrades in the desert returned to his face. "Nah, Harry, I ain't gonna be a punk for the rest of my life. The one thing I've got left is my pride. So we play the game. If I lose, I lose; but I've been a two-bit loser for so long that I think it's about time my luck changed for the better."

"You could have fucking discussed this with me first," Dooks angrily retorted. "We're friends. I deserved to be consulted about this."

Robby smiled crookedly. Then he picked up the opened bottle of whiskey and drank long and deep. "Too late for regrets, bro; the deed's already done. Hey, I suggest we just do like the mutt says and play, till just one of us is left alive."

Dooks looked at Manface. The creature smiled sagely back at him. It said nothing and gave Dooks the impression that it wasn't in any kind of a hurry to be anywhere else anytime soon. This impression was reinforced by the demon's general demeanor; frozen into its Sphinx-like pose like carved anthracite; its body incapable of motion, its misplaced human features redefining the word 'abnormal.'

But appearances could be deceiving. Dooks realized that now. Robby had been the closest person to him for the past six months— his BFF—they had eaten, drunk and even whored together, sharing some of the prostitutes who occasionally crashed at Robby's place— and yet, it was Robby who'd just played him the biggest swerve of his life since he'd lost his job.

Dooks did his best to forgive Robby his self-centeredness and stupidity, but found that he could not.

Instead, he shook his head at the demon. "Sorry, guys, but I'm out of here." He gave Robby a thumbs-down sign, and then shrugged at the grotesque Manface. "I forego my wish. Mutt, you have my blessing to work out whatever deal you like with Robby."

He turned to leave but was restrained by Robby's hand on his shoulder.

"Fucking let go of me, you drunk sonofabitch," Dooks spat while turning around to glare at Robby. "I just told you I'm not having anything more to do with this. You go on with your witchcraft if you want. You can also clean up the mess afterwards."

But then he froze, icy fingers stroking his spine.

Robby was pointing a gun at him. Dooks recognized the gun. The old revolver had belonged to Robby's grandfather and Robby kept it loaded in his nightstand in case of intruders, which, with people entering and leaving his house at all hours of the day and night wasn't really logical. Robby had never fired the gun in Dooks's presence and Dooks had often wondered if the old firearm's mechanism still worked or had grown rusted from age and lack of use.

Hell of a time to find out now, he thought. *Robby looks upset and unhinged enough to shoot me.*

"Sit down, Harry, the game goes on," Robby said coldly.

But Dooks shook his head. "Screw you. I dare you to shoot me. You can't, you idiot, because the gunshot noise would alert the entire motel, and then what explanation would you give for two dead bodies? That we tried to steal your booze? Or maybe, and what the cops are more likely to believe, that you tried to steal our booze; and when we didn't share with you, you offed us both."

Dooks laughed at the frustration on Robby's face, with his friend's body trembling as he realized that except he wanted a one-way trip from here to the slammer, the weapon he held was now completely useless.

"And so once more, adieu to both of you," Dooks intoned solemnly, with his hand on the doorknob. "Right now, I'm going home to sleep. And first thing in the morning I'm packing my bags and leaving your house, Robby, so you don't try to sacrifice me in my sleep in some other ritu—... What the fuck!?"

Dooks had just gotten the motel room door open and now all he could do was stare in surprise and horror.

"Wh-wh-wha-wha . . ."

Both words and logic failed him. Because the outside world seemed to have ceased to exist. Where there had previously been a concrete parking lot, a hedge of shrubs, and the rear wall of the motel's middle block facing Hicks's rear block room, now there was nothing out there.

No, that's not exactly true, Dooks decided as his eyes adjusted to the strange sight. *I'm looking at a logical emptiness. Not an emptiness created by a lack of things, but rather an emptiness that creates a lack of things. What we routinely refer to as 'The Void.'*

Behind him, he heard Robby loudly catch his breath. *So the betraying sonofabitch didn't know this would happen either.*

"Fuck!" Robby gasped in horror, stepping up beside Dooks.

What faced them was an expanse of fathomless and liquid black. The black all seemed to be one shade of darkness, but then, without losing that initial shade of ebony, it seemed to also become many colors, all of them black, and all of them swirling around like water going down a drain.

Dooks was seized with sudden dread, dread that stemmed from the knowledge, the irrefutable knowledge that if he took just one step out of this motel room, one step into the void ahead of him, he would be sucked down into that black whirling funnel, sucked down, down, down into the abyss, until he found himself standing face-to-face with the devil.

Dooks took a cautious step back from the evil void, and then, after a hate-filled look at Robby, he carefully shut the door in both their faces.

"Robert Peter Mayfield, I really should have just shoved you out into that thing," he said quietly as they both turned to stare at Manface.

"What the hell is that outside?" Robby was already asking the demon.

Now the dog-demon laughed. There was something very unnerving about its laughter, and not just the fact of the human face on the canine body.

Damn, Dooks thought with a queasy feeling in the pit of his stomach. *Hicks wasn't about winning any prizes as a pinup model during his lifetime, but now...*

If Hicks had looked ugly in life, his face was grotesque now; and this was compounded by its odd situation.

Just to convince himself he wasn't dreaming, Dooks looked back at Hicks's faceless corpse. But that looked even more like the product of a dream than Robby's transformed dog did, so he once more looked back at the former.

"When you summoned me you also opened up a portal to the void," Manface explained. "For you two at least, the external world no long exists."

"How do we restore things to normal?" Robby asked in a horrified voice.

Dooks knew Robby wasn't faking his fright. He felt exactly the same. With his stomach feeling like it was working out on a trampoline, he nervously glanced back at the door. That thing outside there!

"Yes, how do we put the outside world back where it belongs?" he asked Manface.

"The only way to do so is to complete the ritual. Both of you must finish playing the Devil's Coin Game. Once there is a single winner, things will normalize again."

"What if I refuse to do so?" Dooks asked. "What if I choose to wait the night out?" He gestured at the digital clock near Hicks's television. "The way I see it, mutt, this weird situation of things outside can't continue forever. Sure, it's nighttime now, but Hicks works—I mean *worked*—as the janitor here. Come morning, people are gonna come look for him. I don't think they'll find this room missing then. The room is certain to still be here."

Robby was nodding along to this thread of reasoning. Robby was sweating with fright now.

"Yes, this room will still be here," Manface agreed. "But you two won't be. At the crack of dawn I will return to hell and both of you will be forced to accompany me there." The demon laughed. "Except, of course, the game is completed according to the rules and produces a clear winner."

Dooks stared at the dog-demon, trying to determine if it was bluffing; but the creature's borrowed human visage gave very little away.

There was nothing to do but go on.

"Alright, let's play the game to its conclusion," Dooks agreed, after another disgusted look at Robby, who was having another drink of whiskey. Then he asked, "But what's the procedure now?" Without turning that way, he jerked his thumb at Hicks. "First time around, we each flipped the devil's coin, but now that there's just the two of us remaining, if we play the game the same way, a head-against-tail result will make us equal, with no winner."

Robbie lowered the bottle of whiskey from his lips, belched and then explained: "Dude, this time we pick heads or tails *before* we throw. Whoever the coin favors wins."

Dooks nodded. He'd just realized something that Robby hadn't. Sure, Robby had only begun drinking after they'd offed Hicks, and seemingly due to his current nervousness over the vanished outside world was now drinking heavily—over half of the bourbon in the first bottle was gone now—but Robby still had that fighter's advantage over Dooks. Dooks began praying that Robby hadn't realized that if the outside world no longer existed for both of them, he could simply shoot Dooks if he won, and no one would hear it.

"Let's get on with it," Robby said, angrily dropping the old revolver down on the coffee table, where the gun landed with a thud like a hammer. "It sucks to realize that this is completely useless in here."

Dooks heaved a sigh of relief at his words. He looked around for his knife and discovered it was still stuck in Hicks's belly. He walked over there and with a shiver of revulsion, grabbed the hilt of the knife. He pulled against the faint resistance of clotted blood and stiffening muscle. The knife slid free of its human sheath.

Feeling like a butcher, Dooks stepped up to the edge of the coffee table again. Robby already had his own knife in one hand and the coin in the other. But, on seeing the grim expression on Dooks's face, he put down his knife for a moment, picked up the bottle of Wild Turkey, and drank deeply from it again. When he pulled the mouth of the bottle away from his lips, only about a quarter of the brown liquid remained, sloshing about within its glass confines.

"That really hit the spot," Robby commented. Then he waved the whiskey bottle at Dooks. "Hey, are you sure you don't want a drink first? You might as well—might be the last drink you ever have. We're both condemned men."

Dooks shook his head. He didn't trust himself to reply Robby in any kind of a civil way. *Yes, we're both condemned men . . . and that is your damn fault.* He felt like throttling Robby, felt like leaping over the coffee table and tightening his fingers around the asshole's neck.

Robby nodded tipsily and once more replaced the whiskey bottle on the coffee table and picked up the devil's coin. "Okay, let's play. Remember the rules. We pick heads or tails and then we gag ourselves again and—"

"Don't bother about the gags," Manface interrupted, in a calm, if somewhat amused voice. "In here no one will hear you scream. And I for one love the sound of human screaming—it reminds me of home, where we torture the human damned day and night without pause." The demon laughed again and its rigid black body seemed to glitter with mirth. "In the same way that the outside world no longer exists for the two of you at the moment," it went on after laughing, "so you don't exist for them either. Your army could drop a bomb in here and no one outside would hear the slightest sound."

Dooks cringed when Manface said this. He wished the demon hadn't gone into so much detail. What if Robby remembered the gun?

But clearly, Robby's alcohol consumption had now begun impeding his reasoning. He just nodded at the demon's comments, then turned back to Dooks. "Okay, so where was I? Yeah, Harry, so head or tails, and then we *don't* gag ourselves. I flip the coin and let it fall on the table. Winner wins and loser loses; and our demon friend gets to eat the loser's heart." He pointed the tip of his knife at Dooks. "Ya got that?"

Dooks nodded. "Yeah, I got it, Robby. Heads for me."

"You sure?" Robby asked, pointing at the demon head engraved on the coin's surface. "I'm askin' 'cos Hicks said he didn't like this dude's looks—bad luck for him; and look what's happened to his fat ass. Hey, we're friends, Harry. You can change your mind if you like. If you wanna take tails, I'll accept heads."

Dooks shook his head. "Thanks, but no thanks. I'll stick with heads."

Robby nodded. "Okay, I'm tails then."

Robby flipped the coin. As the coin once more described its slower than usual arc in the air, Dooks felt like his heart had risen up his throat and replaced his tongue in his mouth. The coin spun with seemingly infinite slowness and each of its two and a half revolutions coincided with the thudding of Dooks's heart; heart-beating so loud that Dooks felt certain, despite Manface's assurance that no one could possibly hear any noise they made in here, that all of the motel's guests and everyone else for miles around could hear his fear.

Then the coin landed on the table, flipped over after hitting one of the whiskey bottles, spun for several seconds and lay still next to the grip of Robby's revolver.

Both men crowded over it and stared.

Dooks heart sank. He'd lost, the coin showed 'tails.'

On, seeing the result of the coin toss, Robby instantly snatched up the whiskey bottle and took a good hit. Then he began laughing, waving his knife at Dooks. "Yeah, yeah, yeah! I just knew my bad luck was due for a change tonight. Yeah, I'm a winner, Harry! Finally I'm a fucking winner! YEAH!"

He managed to calm himself a little. "Sorry, Harry, didn't mean to do you dirty like this, bro. I really didn't; but . . . well, you know . . ."

"That's alright," Dooks said calmly. "I forgive you." Then he bent down, dropped his knife on the coffee table and snatched up Robby's revolver. He pointed the gun at Robby's face and fired.

While aiming the gun Dooks had a moment's apprehension. What if it didn't fire?

But it did. There was an ear-rending explosion and the top of Robby's head—most of the skull behind his right eye—blew away.

Robby stood swaying for a few seconds, with the bottle of Wild Turkey in his hand, a surprised look in his bloodshot eyes, and a quarter of his head missing. And then he collapsed to the floor, stone dead.

Breathing heavily, Dooks dropped the gun and picked up his knife again. Then he turned to face the demon Manface.

"We have a winner," he told the demon.

The demon frowned. "This is against the rules of the game. You cheated, Harry. A contestant can't—"

"Shut up, mutt," Dooks said coldly. "Robby betrayed my faith in him and I returned the favor. And besides, from what I hear about you demons, you lot cheat all the time; so don't call the kettle black. So, the way I see it, I fucking won just now."

Manface didn't protest, so Dooks went on: "So, are you gonna eat his heart and grant me my two wishes or what?"

Manface was silent for a few moments. Dooks imagined it was running its mind over the implications of his action. He was worried, but not overly so. For one thing, the demon was the only one here, and it didn't seem like anyone was monitoring it from down below; so itself and himself were the only two who'd know what had really happened here.

But the real thing that set Dooks's mind at ease was how the demon was sneaking glances at Robby's corpse and licking its lips. Dooks could see how desperately it wanted to eat Robby's heart.

Manface finally smiled. "Okay, you have a deal, Harry Dooks. I'll let *how* you won slide. But in return for this you only get one wish, not two. Agreed?"

Dooks hedged. "Hey, why not two? That's cheating!"

The demon laughed. "Maybe it is, but who are *you* to judge me?"

Dooks shrugged. "Yeah, okay, mutt. I came here expecting just one wish anyway." Then he looked shrewdly at the demon. "But no tricks, right? I get exactly what I wish for?"

"Cross my heart, Harry—no, I mean Robby's heart. Now please cut it out of him quickly, before it begins to cool down and loses part of its flavor."

Feeling intense relief for the second time tonight, Dooks got down to the task of extracting Robby's heart from his chest.

CHAPTER 7

Roman

Roman opened up a fresh beer and watched TV. The hooker was still in his bathroom. She'd not flushed the toilet yet so he figured she was still busy on the seat.

He still had his erection.

The television was now showing an interview with a rock band he liked. KCS, or Kimchi Chocolate Stereo. Two Korean-American sisters, the sisters' boyfriends, and their keyboard player. Also present in the interview studio was the band's manager Jojo, older sister to the two in the band.

"So, Lulu, what would you say is your greatest songwriting inspiration?" the interviewer asked.

Lulu laughed like the stoner she was and replied: "Sex? Well, most of the time it is, ya know. How much sex I'm gettin', how much I ain't gettin', how much I think I should be gettin'." She snuggled up closer to her boyfriend Zombie Joe on the long couch the band were sitting on, and added, "Then I discuss my concerns with my bae and we make adjustments."

Roman laughed. The band's latest CD—*The Hour Before U Die*—was his favorite listening at the moment. He'd streamed it all through this current trip. There was just something about the ridiculous level of noise these five managed to make between them, that defied any rational consideration of the world's worries while they were playing.

The toilet flushed. A short while later the bathroom door opened and the hooker walked out.

"Thanks, I really needed to go," she said.

Roman nodded. "It's happened to me more than once. One time I was driving east to Michigan. I don't recall now what I'd eaten for lunch, but . . ." He laughed, then stopped because she didn't appear to be listening to him anymore. Her gaze was fixed on his crotch.

"Hey, you *sure* you don't want some help with that? It's gotta be uncomfortable being hard for so long." She licked her lips. "And in the morning you'll have the bluest balls ever. Blue as the sea."

Roman considered. This woman had a good body, with wide hips and nicely toned legs. He studied her face, trying to penetrate her excessive makeup. He couldn't; her face was a professional mask, her cosmetics applied to achieve a specific effect, just like a clown's makeup was. In her case the result was neither comic nor repulsive, but its attractiveness was entirely painted on. This work-face of hers was a promise, the loud hinting that here before him stood a delightfully sleazy person.

She might even look like Amy under all her warpaint, Roman mused. *Like that girl I initially booked for tonight did. In any case, I can definitely pass the time with her.*

***

Where Roman Fowler was concerned, Amy Watkins was 'the one that got away.' They'd dated for six months, lived together for a year, and then, one fine Sunday morning, Amy was gone.

Roman had been out of town at the time. He'd gotten back to Worcester, MA to find an empty house waiting for him.

Amy had changed her phone numbers so he couldn't locate her online. Her friends had all claimed not to know where she'd gone either. One person said he'd heard Amy had traveled east, to somewhere in South Dakota; someone else had said she'd traveled south to Las Vegas to work as a showgirl; someone else had mentioned Hollywood.

Roman had made several attempts to locate Amy, but had then given up in frustration. When she'd vanished, he had been just days away from buying her an engagement ring. It had seemed impossible to him that the woman he'd been dreaming of spending the rest of his life with no longer wanted him in her life.

That had happened a year ago. Since that time Roman had largely gotten over the hurt and had even resumed dating. But still, each time he saw a women who looked like Amy Watkins, the old feelings resurfaced.

***

"Hey, I got rubbers in my purse if that's what you're concerned about," the prostitute said in a hopeful tone of voice.

Roman pointed his can of beer at her. "Yeah, baby. Sit down and have a Bud with me and let's negotiate."

Pleased, she sat down and after he'd handed her a beer, said, "My name's Christine."

He nodded. "I'm Roman. Pleased to meet you, Christine."

While drinking, Christine adjusted the hem of her already too-short dress with her left hand. She however did so in reverse; rather than smooth the glittering blue fabric down towards her knees, she slid it even closer to her hips, with the effect that when she was done, Roman had a clear view of her uncovered sex. The lips of her vagina mesmerized him as if they were speaking to him; promising him the most wonderful erotic feeling ever.

With her dress properly adjusted to devastating effect, Christine concentrated on watching the KCS interview.

"We're working on a new record now," Zombie Joe was saying. "We're taking inspiration from war and famine and natural disasters, and—"

"And of course, sex," Lulu butted in. "We were gonna call the album *Sex Sex Sex*, but big sis vetoed it."

"I don't want you guys being confused with a bunch of erotic Satan worshippers," band manager Jojo Kim explained. "That kinda gimmick may work for Slain Jane or even Chill Bill, but it isn't right for KCS." Jojo laughed. "You guys catch enough flak already for being *overloud*."

"But that *was* the original plan," keyboard player Doll Face said, "to be the loudest fucking band in the world."

"Yeah, we wanted to make music even the deaf could enjoy," bassist Kiki Kim added, with a laugh. "We ain't there yet; we're still working on it."

Christine looked away from the TV. "You like these guys?" she asked Roman, gesturing sideways at the screen with her beer.

He nodded. "Hard to believe I know, but yes, I do."

Christine scowled. "I tried to get into them once, but damn, they're so fucking noisy. Half the time I can't make out what Lulu Kim is bitchin' about, and when I can understand her, her voice gives me a headache."

"That's precisely the reason *why* I listen to them," Roman told her, laughing. "No, not the headache, but because of how loud they are. I travel a lot by road, and playing them in my car as I drive from state to state seems to make the hours and miles fly by. I dunno, maybe they tranquilize me so I don't notice the time and distance passing."

Roman had been avoiding staring at Christine's exposed vagina. Not because he was embarrassed by it, but because he wanted to finish watching the KCS interview. He had a thing for Jojo Kim, the band's manager and most beautiful of the sisters. (Although he denied that his crush on Jojo had anything to do with his departed Amy Watkins, he admitted to slight similarities between the two women.)

But now that he been distracted from the interview to speak to Christine again, Roman decided to give up. The gaudily-painted prostitute had now carelessly draped one leg over the arm of her armchair, and was now so open to him that he could make out the sweet dark hole in the middle of her blushing genital rose. His manhood strained at the delicious sight and he sighed in defeat and gestured down at his pants. "Christine, baby, what can you do for my penis?" he asked, breathing hard.

She gave him a sly look. "Do you wanna find out there on the couch . . . or on the bed?"

"Bed's better." Roman put down his half-drunk can of beer, got to his feet and extended a hand to Christine. "How much do you charge per hour?"

She was already slipping out of her dress. "Three hundred bucks. But I'll stay the night for a thousand."

Stripped naked, her body was fantastic, but Roman shook his head. "Nah. You're hot, baby, but the money'll be wasted. I just know I'm gonna fall asleep once we're done fucking. Overworked, underpaid, and too drunk to fuck more than twice, that's me."

Christine nodded and waved a strip of condoms at him. "That's fine with me. It's *your* cock, honey."

She led the way to the bed and Roman slipped off his pants and joined her on top of it.

He noticed a long scar on the right side of her belly, extending from the outside of her pelvic bone to her navel. He ran his fingers along the faded red line. "How'd you get this?"

She frowned. "Three years ago I got unlucky. A stoned trick didn't wanna pay me. When I began making a racket, he attacked me with a knife. I woke up in the ICU, thinking the doctors were angels."

"Shit, and I think I've had a hard life."

Christine waved it aside: "Just part of the dangers of a hooker's job. The pay's good and it's less work than slaving my ass away at fucking Walmart. But of course, there's also more chance of running into crazies. Anyway, I survived." She traced the wound with the fingers of her right hand. "It don't hurt anymore, just itches every now and again."

He nodded. Just thinking that someone had dug a knife into Christine hurt Roman, who had never been a violent person. He was a simple, hardworking fellow, who didn't understand why some people felt the need to harm others. He couldn't even watch pro wrestling without wincing at the faked violence. So for him, seeing such a brutal wound on a woman made him a little sad. Maybe he'd have had less of a reaction if the victim had been male; but he doubted it.

Christine, however, had apparently already forgotten about the old wound and its gruesome history. She was sizing up his penis with an expert eye. The way she moistened her lips with her tongue made him wonder how many penises she'd had between them.

"Hard as you are, I doubt you're gonna want any foreplay," she said, ripping up a condom wrapper. "But how do you want me—pussy or ass?"

"Pussy, and get on top. I wanna hold your breasts while we do it. You've got incredible tits."

The compliment clearly pleased her. Her lipstick-plastered mouth cracked open in a broad smile. "Honey, you're the boss, and I'm gonna ride ya like a hoss!" she growled and leapt on top of him.

The rest of it was all very pleasant. It was wonderful. Christine slipped a condom on him and rode him, rode him, rode him with such expertise that afterwards, while slipping the sperm-packed condom off of himself, Roman asked her for her phone number. "I will definitely be needing your physical services next time I'm in Raynham."

Christine gave him her phone number, but then said, "It's not workin' at the moment 'cos I didn't pay my subscription—but I'll get that fixed this week, just for you."

Roman nodded and paid her. He already had the money on hand to pay the escort.

"Hey, your hour ain't up yet," she pointed out while slipping the fifty dollar bills inside her purse. "You wanna go again?"

Roman shook his head. Maybe it was the beer, but he felt too tired for more sex. In fact, at the moment Roman felt tired enough to sleep for two days. There was something really odd about how tired he felt.

Christine kissed him on his soft penis. In return, he stroked her scar again. And, while tracing the faded red line from her navel to her hip, he had the feeling that she'd not told him the whole truth about how she'd come by the wound. In fact, he felt she'd not told him any of the truth at all. But that could wait. He had her phone number and would definitely be hiring her again. He felt certain that once they knew each other a little better, Christine would readily tell him the truth about how she'd gotten that old wound.

"Another job well done," Christine remarked brightly, grinning at him. "I'll expect to hear from you soonest, honey."

"Oh you will. Count on it."

She slipped back into her blue dress and high heels, and left.

Roman sighed happily and fell asleep.

CHAPTER 8

Mandy & Tenebra

When Mandy Cherry regained consciousness again, she was tied up on Tenebra's couch. She had a slight headache from stunning herself. She was arranged in a sitting position and her hands were bound behind her back; but her feet were free. She had been stripped of all her clothes.

Mandy wasn't gagged. She put this down to Tenebra's knowing she wouldn't dare scream for help; not with two fresh corpses in the room that she wouldn't be able to explain, and that footage of Dewdrop beheading one of them on her cellphone.

As to her own killing of Dewdrop, Tenebra could easily claim self-defense. She would go free and Mandy would go to jail for a very long time.

But she hasn't called the cops yet. Why not? Part of it must be because she was blackmailing Petra—that's illegal too—but maybe there's more to it than that.

Mandy repressed the fright that threatened to overwhelm her. *Dammit, things sure went downhill fast tonight!*

Tenebra was sitting opposite her on the coffee table. She wasn't looking Mandy's way at the moment, but was instead staring at the TV, which was playing a car insurance commercial. She didn't appear aware that Mandy had regained consciousness. Mandy wished she could sneak out of the motel room while her captor's back was turned, but with her hands tied behind her, she doubted she could even get to her feet without alerting Tenebra.

She began looking around, assessing her current situation; trying to figure out how to escape.

The headless woman stood by the wall, with her arms by her sides, and her head on the rug by her feet. She was a horrible sight to behold, with that brutally truncated neck, and blood caked down the front of her nightie. Mandy's problem with her wasn't that she was dead, but that Tenebra had somehow brought her back to life again; had reanimated her. Other than standing upright, the corpse wasn't moving in any way. But corpses weren't even supposed to be able to stand up unaided.

She's a zombie now!

The sight of the zombie woman made Mandy want to start screaming in horror.

Seeing the reanimated woman was horrible enough, but Dewdrop's corpse lay opposite her on the other side of the room, beneath the window. Just like Mandy, Dewdrop had been stripped completely naked. Her face was frozen in her death expression, her eyes and mouth expressing her intense surprise at the sudden unexpected pain that had struck her from behind. And that hole in her chest . . . rimmed by a circle of dried blood.

Mandy tried to work out how long she'd been unconscious for. *Stripping both of us naked would have taken her about ten minutes . . . or more since she also moved Dewdrop's body, but maybe she had her zombie helper do that . . . Hey, the TV . . . what program was she watching? . . . The sci-fi flick was just ending, so I can't . . .*

Tenebra turned on the coffee table and saw that she was awake.

"Hey there," Tenebra said. "I was gonna wake you once I finished my preparations, but now you can watch them too." Then her eyes turned icy cold and she waved the black knife she had killed Dewdrop with at Mandy. "Now listen, you and I are gonna rap. Don't even think of screaming for help. One squeak from you and I'll ram this blade so far up your cunt, you'll think I'm operating on your throat."

Mandy quickly nodded her agreement to the conditions for their conversation. She now got her first really good look at the real Tenebra. *How the hell could we have been so wrong?* She instinctively looked sideways at the headless woman, and then looked down at her severed head on the floor. Then, after studying the dead face for a few seconds, she looked back up at Tenebra, trying to work out the similarities and differences.

There was little to choose from between the two women, the living and the living dead.

Tenebra watched her watch her, not speaking, her eyes saying volumes. She had changed out of her dress while Mandy was unconscious and instead now wore a black tee shirt and black thong. Her black tee shirt was decorated with a large silver pentagram. Her feet were bare, revealing silver toenails. Silver fingernails too. Black and red eyeshadow, like the decoy still wore—lips so darkened that her mouth looked like a black hole. One hand held the black knife; the other gripped three fat red candles. A box of similar candles, both red and black, lay on the coffee table. The box also contained a few other things that Mandy couldn't identify.

The black amulet shaped like a devil's head dangled between Tenebra' breasts.

Mandy recalled that Tenebra had spoken of intending to wake her up after she'd gotten through with making 'preparations.' She dreaded discovering exactly what those preparations were.

"Who was she?" she asked, pointing at the headless woman with her foot, and finally getting a grip on her fear of the unknown forces that had brought her back to her current semblance of life.

"A hooker I met yesterday; her name's Kelli. I hired her for sex and then, realizing we looked a bit similar, I offered her extra money to impersonate me when you got here."

Mandy scowled. "I should have spotted the difference."

Tenebra smiled coldly. "You couldn't have. Kelli and I are about the same height, same weight, same hairdo . . . except for the color of our eyes, and"—she pushed back the hair over her left ear—"what your dead girlfriend noticed: the number of ear piercings. She was quite older than me, but the black makeup hid that." Tenebra got to her feet. "I figured that being in a hurry, you were certain to mistake one goth chick for another."

"You expected a double-cross then?" Mandy was stalling for time. Behind her, her fingers had just snagged the end of the cord Tenebra had bound her wrists with. Mandy felt confident she could work free of the cord. But to do so, she needed time. And so she had to keep Tenebra talking. "You expected Petra Velli to double-cross you?"

"Never trust a mobster's wife," Tenebra said, with a sour look on her face. "Petra could pay me five times what I asked for and not notice it was gone—Marko might as well be the US mint—but she's a bitch, plain and simple."

Suddenly Tenebra looked amused. "You know, we lesbians really should stick together. If we followed that simple golden rule, you for instance, wouldn't find yourself in the situation you're in now.

"You're a hypocrite. You started all this by blackmailing Petra."

Tenebra nodded. "Yeah, you got me there. Guilty as charged. But Petra has so much fucking money. What I asked her for isn't even peanuts. Two hundred grand is less than she uses to order her designer douche from overseas."

"That doesn't make blackmail right."

"Trying to kill me is even wronger," Tenebra said. "And now unfortunately, you're gonna pay the price."

Tenebra paused for a moment and then said, "Oh yes, and thank you for bringing me my amulet."

Mandy admitted her curiosity: "What's the big deal about it anyway? It's such an ugly piece of jewelry. Why insist we had to bring it with us?"

Tenebra sighed wistfully and fondled the demonic-looking pendant like it was a sensitive part of a lover's body. "I don't require it for this present ritual, if that's what you're wondering," she replied. "This amulet has incredible sentimental value for me, that's all. I could never bear thinking of it being in the possession of someone I have fallen out of love with."

Mandy could not resist mocking her: "It must have seen a lot of going back and forth then."

Tenebra's mouth tightened up in displeasure, and she waved her black knife at her captive. "Watch your words before I stab you somewhere excruciating, like up your asshole."

Mandy, who had been about to make a few more acid comments about Tenebra's love life, took the threat seriously and instead ate her insults before she was forced to do so.

By now she'd gotten a good grip on the loose cord by her wrists. It was thin and felt like a shoelace. She began carefully working at it, her right hand fingers managing to snare a loop of the cord that was not tied tightly, and then with her left hand she slid the free end back through that loop, loosening it, which immediately resulted in a lessening of the painful tension around her wrists. Mandy could already feel that the cord was much slacker and now would require very little effort to get free of.

That's better, she thought. *I just need to keep talking to this witch and hope she doesn't notice what I'm doing.*

It took her an effort to hide her delight at her progress and continue to present a worried face to Tenebra.

"You know," Tenebra said, unexpectedly changing the subject with a wistful look on her face. "Life is a constant trade between what you have and what you want. Take me, for instance. At one time I had a boyfriend who really loved me and wanted to marry me. But I also had secrets: my guy didn't know that I also liked women, liked them as much as I like men; and he also had no idea I was into the black arts." She giggled at Mandy. "By black arts, I mean magic, not hip-hop; though Chill Bill Wachowski gets me wetter than the rain does. So, anyway, I had a choice to make, between a guaranteed love or my unfulfilled desires. I chose desire. Desire for pussy, desire for power . . . desire for the opportunity to fulfil my desires. . . . One benefit pussy has over cock is, you never have to swallow or brush your teeth afterwards. Though you may need to floss if the girl doesn't trim her bush often."

Mandy nodded like a dutiful pupil. Despite her current straits she found herself wondering (and not for the first time) at the modern profusion of bisexual, biromantic, and pansexual 'lesbians.' How exactly did a woman consider herself a 'lesbian' if she also liked men?

She knew that in the bad old days for homosexuality, lesbians had gotten married because they were forced to conform to society's mores. If you stood out you were persecuted, and the easiest way to not be considered a sexual deviant was to have a man by your side.

But nowadays?

It was crazy how no one seemed to like 'just girls' anymore. She knew too many so-called lesbians who took off once a month with men, as if they were taking menstrual medication. The commonest excuse for this behavior was that they had gotten drunk and one thing had led to another; and besides, they had no recollection of what happened anyway, so no real harm had been done to their non-binary sexuality. As far as Mandy could tell, those girls were all having sex with boys simply to ensure they weren't 'missing out' on something crucial for one to be considered properly feminine.

She viewed her current situation as a case in point. Of the five women involved in it—herself, Dewdrop, Petra Velli, Tenebra . . . and of course, decapitated Kelli—she, Amanda Sheryl Collins, was the only one of them who was entirely lesbian in her sexual orientation, as all of the other four women were either currently sexually involved with men, or had been sexually entangled with them at some point in their past. (To all appearances Petra Velli was *happily* married. Dewdrop had both been abused by her father and also *willingly* worked as a prostitute, and Kelli was/had been a prostitute. And here was Tenebra admitting now how she'd once been *in love* with some man.)

So is it that lesbianism is less satisfying than it once was; or were all these women into the same sex scene just because it seemed edgy and made them stand out? Or for them is lesbianism simply a way to hit back at their ex-boyfriends or religious parents?

"So long as you're happy," she replied Tenebra now; trying not to anger her with a perceived lack of empathy. "I don't see that it matters. You're young and beautiful and have the world at your feet. What else matters? O.K., so you broke up with Petra Velli, but there's lots of other rich women . . . and men, who'll give their right arm or leg to have you as a trophy wife."

"Flattery will get you nowhere," Tenebra replied. "It definitely won't make me untie you. You still have to pay the price for trying to kill me."

"So . . . what do you intend to do with me?" Mandy asked in pretend fright. "Is it really too much for us to just let bygones be bygones and part as friends?" She faked as seductive a face as she could manage. "Or maybe, seeing as we're both LGBT, we could even become lovers."

Ugh! In reality, sleeping with Tenebra was the furthest thing on Mandy's mind. She would rather have sex with a snake; or . . . heaven forbid, with a man, something she considered as repulsive as fat girls eating tapeworms to lose weight. Mandy just wanted to be as far away from here as possible.

Her wrists were almost free now, and she felt confident she could escape the room, but for the problem of the zombie woman who had thwarted her previous escape attempt.

The headless woman stood there as immobile as if she was carved from rock, and yet Mandy knew that at a single command from Tenebra, that motionless corpse would come to life and attempt to stop her; somehow seeing without eyes; or maybe, she still saw through the dead orbs in her severed head.

"What's going to happen to me?" Mandy questioned again.

"I am going to sacrifice you to open up a portal to hell," Tenebra replied in an excited voice.

"What? Are you nuts?" Mandy asked, her horror only half faked.

"Yeah, you heard me right. I'm going to kill you here in this room, and in this same motel room a portal to hell will open up and I will walk through it."

"You are completely insane," Mandy gasped, suddenly feeling very worried; for two reasons. Firstly, because Tenebra had now begun waving the black knife at her and making swift sawing motions with it that came scarily close to Mandy's neck; and secondly, because her attempt to finally break free of the cord around her wrists had just stalled at an extremely stubborn knot, which paradoxically appeared to be the final knot she needed to loosen, but which, possibly because it has been tied first, had been done up much tighter than the others.

"It's okay if you think I'm insane," Tenebra said evenly. "But you know you're lying to yourself when you say that."

"I'm not saying you're insane because you want to open a door to hell," Mandy explained, while her entire naked body broke out in a cold sweat as she desperately tried to work the final knot loose before Tenebra tired of conversation and commenced stabbing her instead. "I don't doubt that you can do what you say. What I mean is, why would anyone want to go to *hell* . . . of all sucky places?"

"I'm a witch, hell is home to me."

Mandy rolled her eyes. "So what? I'm from Dresden, Ohio, and I hate the fucking place." Unable to resist the lure of bad memory, she laughed. "You would too if you're from around there: my mum wants me to come home and marry the boy next door, who I know is gay. My dad wants me to become a schoolteacher, chasing brats around. Meanwhile, my uncle Vincent wants me to join his drug business. When I say 'drug business,' I mean narcotics, not running the family drugstore."

"And so, to escape your family, you decided to take the upright path and become a hitwoman."

"It sounds really nasty when you put it like that," Mandy agreed, relieved now that she had gotten free of that final troublesome knot. "But most folks I've killed deserved to die anyway, so really I'm doing a public service."

"People like me?" Tenebra asked sweetly. "Did you ever stop to consider that in some cases your employers might be lying to you? Or might themselves need killing?"

"I just followed the money," Mandy said. "It's the American way. It's called 'free enterprise.' "

She figured she deserved the disgusted look Tenebra flung her after that comment.

All I need now is to choose my moment wisely. In the meantime I need to keep this bitch talking. I also need something to attack her with. I don't dare take her on with that knife pointing right at me and her zombie minion watching. And where the hell did she put my cellphone? I don't see it anywhere.

"Listen, Tenebra," she said. "You can't kill me anyway. An eyewitness saw me and Dewdrop driving over to your room."

Mandy said this purely to buy time. As long as that video of Dewdrop murdering Kelli was on her cellphone, any eyewitness testimony would merely serve to corroborate her guilt.

She was glad to see however that Tenebra took the bait. "Someone saw you arrive here? who?"

"It was a hooker."

"A prostitute? What did she look like?"

Mandy didn't think it mattered if she told Tenebra the truth: "Hookers all look the same to me; like buckets of sleaze and disease. But she was wearing a short, shiny blue dress and blue shoes. The most striking thing about her was the amount of makeup she had on. It was more than excessive. So much I couldn't tell what her face looked like under it"

"Did she tell you her name?"

"No, I didn't ask."

Mandy was surprised when Tenebra smiled at her. It was neither a gloating smile nor one of victory, but rather a sad smile. A pitying smile even, one that gave Mandy a feeling like having an infestation of giant worms in her belly.

"Why the hell are you looking at me like that? Like a mourner at my funeral?"

Tenebra sighed. "Because tonight *is* your funeral. Girl, you couldn't have chosen a worse night to come here. That prostitute you just encountered was Christine Valona."

"Christine Valona. So what's that to me?"

Mandy felt quite confident now, and this was reflected in her conversation with Tenebra. With her hands now free, all she needed now was for Tenebra to turn around for whatever reason, then she could attack her (maybe even kill her as payback for her killing Dewdrop) and escape.

Of course I have to find my clothes and my cell phone first. She thought she felt her clothes down on the floor by her feet, but since she hadn't leaned up from the couch yet, could not be certain of their position there. "Yes, what does the prostitute Christine have to do with me? I met her for the first time tonight."

Tenebra smiled that same sad smile again.

"Well, for one thing, Christine Valona is *dead*," she replied evenly. "For another thing, tonight is the third anniversary of the night she was brutally murdered here in this motel." She laughed. "And last of all and what concerns you is this—since her death Christine has been under a curse. Or maybe it would be more accurate to say that now Christine Valona *is* a curse. She appears here at the motel infrequently, but always shows up on the anniversary of her death. And anyone who sees her whenever she appears dies before morning. That is a guarantee; no one ever sees Christine and lives through the night."

Mandy fought down the fear that attempted to consume her. She remembered how she had felt on encountering the prostitute— Christine—at the corner of the front block. She also recalled the suddenness of the woman's appearance; back then she might have materialized out of thin air even. But of course back then Mandy would never have accepted that that had been the case, she would have put down any abnormalities in Christine's appearance to being a trick of the night, or have thought her mind was playing tricks on her.

On the bright side of her escape attempt, the outer edge of her left foot had just brushed against something that was cold, flat, and hard.

Dewdrop's knife!

As far as she could determine with just her toes, however, the hilt of the knife lay around the edge of the couch; she would be unable to reach it except she was sitting up and looking that way. Which meant that leaping up and surprising Tenebra was out of the question; the witch lady would be on top of her before she could retrieve the knife. So more patience was required; more pretense; more seeming to have meekly accepted her role as sacrificial lamb.

"Stop trying to scare me, bitch," she told Tenebra testily. "You're already gonna kill me, so why try to frighten me as well? That story about Christine is nothing but an urban legend. Every town has those."

"I'm not trying to scare you. Even if *I* don't kill you, you'll be dead before dawn anyway."

Mandy once more fought-down the resurgence of her fear. "So prove it; let me go and then we'll see how true your story is."

Tenebra shook her head. "Sorry, but no can do. Like I was explaining, I need you to open my gateway to hell."

I'm going to send YOU to hell, Mandy thought angrily, pissed off that anyone would think so little of her as to try to use her as a key to unlock their evil front door.

Then she asked, "What's Christine's story anyway? How did she die? Who murdered her and why?"

"Oh, Christine was a hooker, but you already knew that," Tenebra explained. "The reason she applied so much makeup was because she had burnt her face as a teenager. I think she fell asleep while smoking a joint, and set her pillow on fire."

"Guess that's better than burning down the whole house like my friend's cousin Lucy did back in Dresden." She laughed. "I already told you the place is a shit village, right? But occasionally something happens to lighten the boredom. In this case, Lucy, who was dating my Uncle Vince's son Tommy—they were teens then—Lucy set her parents' house on fire while tripping, then she ran away from home."

"Whatever." Tenebra waved her knife at her, threatening her with violence if she didn't keep quiet. "Anyhow, the left side of Christine's face was badly scarred, really really badly, so she used huge amounts of makeup to cover it up—as much as a Japanese geisha would wear; I think the Orient's where she got the concept from."

"Don't go into details, I saw her. She looked grotesque, as garish as a psychedelic wall."

"Funny thing is, the makeup didn't hurt her popularity; she had no shortage of customers; she was reputedly a fantastic fuck. Everyone who slept with her wanted a second helping."

"Good for her. So, who killed her then, and why?"

"Christine Valona got greedy. It's a normal failing with prostitutes; put them near a stash of money and they tend to help themselves to it. In Christine's case she stole a million dollars, a briefcase full of money that belonged to a Brooklyn drug lord named Huggers. That happened over in Springfield. Christine fled here to Raynham and the Sunflower Motel, and Huggers' goons trailed her, found her here, and butchered her." Tenebra frowned. "Something went wrong though, because the goons killed her *before* she'd told them where she'd cached the money."

Mandy laughed. "So you're saying that even though they killed Christine, they never found the million dollars?"

Tenebra nodded. "That's right. The money is still missing. Legend has it that Christine hid it here in this motel, which may explain why she still haunts the place: she's protecting her stash."

"Yeah, right. Even assuming the story about the money is true, how would that mean that anyone she sees now will die that night?"

Now it was Tenebra's turn to laugh. "Well, the story goes that after Christine died she went to hell. But once down there, the devil made a deal with her. He sent her back here to collect six hundred and sixty-six souls for him, after which he would make her a demoness and his personal mistress; apparently rumors of Christine's sexual prowess had gotten down below too. And as you can imagine, Christine found that offer way better than being tortured for all eternity; so she's collecting all the unfortunate souls she can get."

After saying this Tenebra stared pointedly at Mandy. "So now you know. Believe it or not, you're a dead girl, a *very* dead girl. As dead as . . ." She gestured with her handfuls of candles and knife at the two corpses in the room.

Mandy almost attacked her then, when her guard was down and her arms were both thrust out sideways, one pointing towards Dewdrop and the other at the headless woman. But then she noticed the zombie twitch slightly when Tenebra's handful of red candles were aimed at her, and so she cautioned herself to be patient. She needed her clothes. In addition to the fact that her car keys were in a pocket of her jacket, she couldn't simply run outside naked in the middle of the night. She would have a hell of a time explaining herself if the State Police stopped her while driving like that.

"Well, I'm glad you believe that bullshit, because that's all it is," she coldly informed Tenebra. "It's as stupid as that Raynham urban legend of Brainchew that Dewdrop and I heard up at the truck stop yesterday. How soon do you intend to kill me anyway?"

"Don't be in a hurry to die. Hell is a nasty place," Tenebra replied. She fingered the amulet hung around her neck. "I'll get round to killing you once I'm through with my preparations."

Yeah, of course you will, witch. Like I intend to hang around until then.

And then what Mandy had been waiting for happened:

"Alright, let's get started, shall we?" said Tenebra. She then turned away from Mandy towards Dewdrop.

Once certain that Tenebra would not immediately turn around again, Mandy went into action. She leaned forward slowly, her first point of call to retrieve the knife by her foot.

Once she had the knife in hand, she quickly glanced first at the headless zombie standing by the wall and then at Tenebra. Tenebra was humming a song. Mandy recognized the tune; she didn't know its title, but it was something by that incredibly talented rapper Chill Bill Wachowski. Tenebra seemed distracted enough for the moment and so Mandy quickly gathered her clothes too, all of which were strewn on the rug along the front of the couch, with her incriminating cellphone sticking out of a pocket of her jacket.

Her relief at finding her clothes was however completely shattered when she realized Tenebra hadn't neatly removed the clothes from her body, but rather had sliced them off of her, and that what she was currently gathering was actually a collection of rags. Even her panties and bra were shredded.

In a sort of shock she silently retrieved both her cellphone and the keys to the car from what remained of her jacket.

Now she began getting really angry.

Mandy had had no intention of trying to get dressed before leaving the motel room, but still she felt intense rage building in her at the realization that now she would have to flee naked, even if it was just across the short distance from the room to her rented car.

It was partly this anger that got the better of her, and made her charge at Tenebra. Yes, she had intended to attack and possibly kill the woman, but the knowledge that her enforced nudity must now endure for much longer pushed reason to the back of her mind, and caused her to charge like a lioness, rather than creeping up on her prey like a pantheress.

The result of this decision was that in her haste to reach Tenebra (who was bent forward over Dewdrop's corpse) Mandy struck her left knee against the side of the coffee table and so alerted Tenebra to her attack.

Tenebra spun around fast. When her body shifted, Mandy's attack received a further setback when she saw what Tenebra had been doing to her girlfriend's body. It looked like she was carving a pentagram into Dewdrop's belly.

This sight incensed Mandy further, and at the same time made her attack more sloppy; so that now, instead of attacking with pinpoint accuracy like she normally did, she swung the knife wildly, missing Tenebra's neck and instead barely grazing her shoulder.

After the briefest of pauses to assess the damage she had caused, Mandy stabbed at Tenebra again.

Once more she aimed for her opponent's throat, but by now Tenebra had recovered from her initial surprise at seeing her captive free. The goth woman both got her arm up in time to block Mandy's thrust, and also made a counterthrust of her own, which, as the black blade grazed Mandy's ribs gave her major cause for concern about her own safety in this conflict. Yes, she obviously had more fighting experience than Tenebra did, but Tenebra held the longer knife; and Mandy saw no point in hanging around when she had a good chance of escaping alive.

But still, she had one more important thing to take care of before she would feel safe enough to head for the door.

Up to this point (possibly because they had been fighting for less than half a minute) it had seemingly not occurred to Tenebra to summon her zombie to her aid.

Mandy figured there was only one surefire way to prevent that from happening.

That decided, she crouched slightly, opened up her left hand and let her cellphone and car keys drop to the floor. She doubted that Tenebra even noticed what she had just done.

She was still holding the knife in her right hand and stabbing at Tenebra, who was so intent on defending against it that she didn't realize until it was too late what Mandy was up to.

Mandy feinted a knife thrust at her, and when Tenebra parried it, she stepped inside her guard and slammed her left fist hard against the right side of Tenebra's jaw.

The result was exactly what Mandy had planned for and expected: her eyes suddenly glassy, Tenebra dropped like a rock down onto Dewdrop's body. She lay there, trying to move her lips but making no sound.

Mandy decided it was time to leave. She considered finishing Tenebra off, but then thought better of it. Whether by accident or some evil instinct of self-preservation, Tenebra had landed on her back, holding the black knife pointed upwards. Even though she looked like she had just been KO'd in a championship boxing bout,

Mandy knew appearances could be very deceiving. Tenebra did not look like it, but she might be playing possum.

A glance across at the opposite wall of the room revealed that the headless woman was still motionless.

That's good enough!

Mandy decided to cut her losses and run, and that is exactly what she did. She retrieved the cellphone and car keys from the floor and quickly headed for the door.

She felt intense relief once she was outside the motel room, and a cool breeze blew across her bare body. She left the door open, not because she wanted to make it easier for Tenebra to pursue her, but because she wanted to keep her eye on the zombie woman in case she started moving before she reached her car, which would be her signal to start running.

But Mandy soon realized that leaving the door open was actually pointless because Tenebra's own car was in the way, and once she stepped beyond it the open door would be out of view.

However, she only realized this when she was already by the driver's door of Tenebra's green Kia. And by then she had two more reasons not to retreat and shut the door to Room 13.

The first reason was because she was aware of the danger of Tenebra ambushing her and capturing her again.

The second reason was because there was someone standing by the door of the car she was headed for.

That person was (Mandy drew in a gulp of surprised and horrified breath) the supposedly dead prostitute Christine Valona.

Oh fuck! What the hell is she doing here?

The tall tale Tenebra had told her flooded her mind with fear and she almost abandoned her car and set off running for the motel's reception building.

But she remembered that she was naked, and so even if she threw away her bloody knife before she reached the reception lobby, it would be almost impossible to explain herself without prompting some kind of investigation into her story.

And besides, I don't actually believe Tenebra's story. This woman opposite me isn't a ghost. She's as flesh and blood as I am, and I'm going to prove it.

With that in mind and her courage returning (prompted in large part by the return of her anger against Tenebra), Mandy stalked towards the woman standing beside her rented Honda Accord.

"Hey, where's your girlfriend?" Christine asked as she neared her. "You girls were late for our date and so I decided to come and investigate."

"Yeah, you and the fucking cops," Mandy hissed at her. "Listen, something came up. Date's off. Maybe next time."

Mandy no longer felt scared of the woman. *Tenebra is just a nasty person. What was she playing at, trying to scare me like that?*

Meanwhile, however, Christine wasn't moving from her position beside the car door. And Mandy needed her to get out of the way so she could get into the car.

"Move, wilya? I'm in a hurry!" she whispered angrily.

But Christine remained in place by the door and replied in a whisper too. "Not before . . . Look, we had a deal and I really need the money." A bright smile cracked her garish makeup. "Hey, how 'bout if we do it on your backseat? I'll lick your pussy so good it'll ask me for my phone number."

Mandy shook her head. "Lady, are you nuts? Can't you see I'm naked?"

"Naked is great; it makes sex much easier."

"Get the hell out of my way!"

Mandy wanted to scream the words but she was forced to whisper loudly. She would have loved to be able to kill this overly made-up woman and dump her body in the trunk of the car, but she didn't dare. This bitch hooker would very likely scream her head off if she stabbed her.

Mandy's biggest worry was that, at any moment now, Tenebra and her headless minion were going to step out of the motel room and come after her.

But so far that hadn't happened. Mandy figured Tenebra must have a glass jaw. *The witch is out for the count; maybe I should have waited and killed her. But it's too late to go back inside and do it now.*

"Hey, honey, come have a taste!" Christina was now flashing her breasts at Mandy. "Or, don't you think I'm pretty enough for you? You're definitely pretty enough for me. Ooh, girl, your naked body gets me so fucking wet." She began rubbing herself between the legs, the sight of which made Mandy cringe.

Mandy roughly shoved Christine aside, so that Christine staggered over to the trunk end of the car. When Christine regained her balance Mandy waved the knife at her. "Stay away from me, or else . . ."

She figured this should prove sufficient of a deterrent, but Christine was already walking back towards her, with a determined look on her face.

"Fuck you. If you don't fuck me, you ain't fucking leaving here."

She in turn shoved Mandy out of the way and once more blocked off the car door.

Despite Christine Valona's solidity, there was something in her eyes and her voice now that once more brought Tenebra's tale about her to Mandy's mind.

Fear again threatened to overwhelm Mandy. She overwhelmed the fear with anger. After taking a deep breath and thinking, *Okay, lady, we'll see how much of a ghost you are now!* she stabbed Christine in the belly. She stabbed the woman once, twice, and a third time and then left the knife stuck in her body.

Let her wander off and die somewhere; I'm out of here. She was too enraged to care that leaving the knife in the woman's body meant she would be leaving behind evidence that could convict her.

Mandy reached around Christine to open the car door and shove her out of the way again, but to her horror the wounded prostitute still did not relinquish her position by the car door. Yes, she gripped her belly; yes, she gripped the hilt of the knife that now protruded from her belly; but no, she was not bleeding, nor did she appear in any way hurt.

Oh no . . . Fuck!

Mandy now realized that Tenebra had told her the truth about Christine Valona. Christine Valona was fucking dead, a ghost. Mandy also now understood that the real reason Tenebra hadn't pursued her out of her motel room was because she knew Christine was outside here and she didn't dare look at her.

Mandy turned to run away from the ghost, to flee down the concrete aisle between the motel blocks. But Christine had a firm grip on her elbow and even though Mandy beat on her arm as hard as she could, Christine wasn't letting go.

"Please, please, oh my God, please," Mandy pleaded in a soft and terrified voice.

"I tried to be nice to you," Christine said coldly, spinning Mandy around so she faced her again. "You're going to die tonight anyway, and I figured having some great sex before your death would prevent you regretting the shortness of your life. Your evil soul already belongs to my master Lucifer, but a little pleasure for us both before your departure would have been nice." She shook her head disgustedly. "But you're simply not worth it. And so back to your doom you go."

There was something impossible to describe in Christine Valona's face. Mandy had the scary impression that Christine's flesh was fading away to reveal the bones of her skull and then reappearing again. She stood frozen in front of the ghost, with her mind reeling at the impossibility of everything happening to her; and the dread of what Christine was about to do to her. The unforgiving look in the dead hooker's eyes was the most chilling thing Mandy had ever seen.

The knife was still sticking out of Christine's belly, and now she pulled it out with the hand that wasn't restraining Mandy. Expecting to be stabbed as payback, Mandy tensed as the knife came bloodlessly free of Christine's party dress, leaving no tear in the shimmering blue fabric.

She relaxed when Christine threw the knife down onto the cement just as a drizzle began, the drops of water falling with the lightness of displaced autumn leaves.

But then the ghost placed both of her hands on Mandy's breasts. Even though under other situations, two women standing close to one another with their breasts bared may have had erotic connotations, this was nothing like that. Christine's fingers felt like graveworms on Mandy's breasts, like the caress of Death's cold hands.

"Goodbye, girl," Christine told her and gave her a violent shove.

And next, without understanding in the least how it was possible, Mandy found herself flying backwards through the air. She traveled fast, and almost before she realized she was in motion she was zooming over the top of Tenebra's car.

"Oh shit, no!" she moaned as the roof of the green sedan bumped her heels.

"God damn you, Christine!" she gasped next as she went streaking back through the motel room door she'd just exited and left open.

Thankfully, Mandy didn't crash into the floor or coffee table, but instead streaked across the room and slammed full-body into the headless woman. Half-unconscious she dropped to the floor and the zombie dropped on top of her.

Totally unable to move for the moment, Mandy helplessly peeked through half-closed eyes. She watched while Tenebra, who took great care to not look outside the room, shut the door and put the chain on again.

Then Tenebra crossed the room to Mandy and crouched down next to her.

"Welcome back to hell," she said, with a grim smile. "I already told you, girl—your death tonight is kismet."

She said something to the headless woman, who then got up off Mandy and began pulling her to her feet.

Mandy passed out again in the zombie's arms.

CHAPTER 9

Dooks

Extracting Robby's heart from his chest took Dooks only about a third of the time that performing the same procedure on Hicks had. This time Dooks knew exactly what to do, although he cringed while doing it.

He'd cut open Robby's shirt and then cut him open too, two cuts in the belly; one vertical from ribs to crotch, and the second directly under the ribs. That way he could peel most of the abdominal wall back, and once he'd gotten Robby's stomach and small intestines out of the way, cut with relative ease through the diaphragm and spongy lung tissue.

While working he was aware of Manface's hungry glances at his back, but thankfully the demon only watched, it didn't offer advice on how to butcher the corpse like Robby had done with Hicks.

No matter how one views it, slicing up a human body is a queasy task. How the heck do undertakers manage? How do they deal with the smell of blood? This room now reeks like, reeks like . . .

The one thing Dooks avoided doing while opening Robby's belly and digging upward into his chest, was staring at his face. He hated seeing what the bullet had done to the guy's head. Dooks was cutting Robby up where he'd dropped after being shot and there was a bloody mess around Robby's head; destroyed brain matter and skull and scattered brown hair, and a bright pool of blood that extended back into the bathroom. The original gore splatter that marked Robby's death decorated the motel wall next to them.

It was a nasty task to perform for a second time tonight, but Harry Dooks knew he had no choice but to go through with it. The alternative? There was no alternative. Dooks glanced at the door and recalled vividly the swirling formless darkness that now existed outside of the motel room—with the rest of the world seemingly 'set aside' for the moment. Or was it the opposite that had happened: himself and Manface becoming cut off from the world? Whichever it was—either this room or the Earth gone missing—the end result was the same. He was currently adrift in hell's limbo and desperately needed to reconnect with existence as he knew it. (Being 'lost in space and time' like this was the scariest thing that had ever happened to him; much scarier even that having to play the Devil's Coin Game twice.)

Getting back to that logical reality, surviving tonight, was the highest priority he'd ever had.

And since the sole way to get back home was slicing into Robby; so be it. This was Robby's damn fault anyway.

The confused look on Robby's face made Dooks face the fact of his own mortality. He disliked thinking like that and so concentrated on making his second pool of blood around Robby's torso. As he'd expected, by the time he was done, he was twice as bloody as previously.

Once he'd gotten Robby's heart out in one piece he offered it to the demon. He was still crouching, which made his knees ache, and was confused as to where to put the heart: beside Manface, or down on the rug next to the couch? As far as he could see, since the dog-demon was frozen stiff, both options created problems for the creature to eat the heart.

The demon itself said nothing; though it was salivating with anticipation.

There is no way in hell I'm gonna feed it bite by bite, Dooks thought. *If I hold Robby's heart close to its mouth, it looks hungry enough to accidentally begin eating my hand.*

Finally he placed the extracted organ on the coffee table, pulled the table up close to the couch, and then stepped back and watched to see what would happen.

Dooks's mental query as to how Manface would manage to eat the heart was quickly answered. The demon somehow elongated its neck till it looked like a small black giraffe and then chomped into the steaming red lump of human meat. Though it still maintained Hicks's face, its teeth had become long and sharp; and the former illusion that some humanity existed in the creature was thus totally shattered.

Manface's teeth cut into Robby's heart like razors. Dooks felt sick watching it. Whether triggered by the room's current morbid state, or by liquids he'd drunk earlier, he also felt a strong urge to urinate. He almost headed for the bathroom to do so, but the pool of blood from

Robby's head was inside the bathroom too and Dooks didn't feel like stepping in it.

The urge to pee wasn't yet unbearable and he figured he could wait maybe another half hour or so before relieving himself.

But what to do with himself while the demon fed? It was creepy enough watching those unnatural jaws chomp into the meat, but also, Manface was eating at a leisurely pace; like it had all the time in the world.

Then, from the equally unnatural silence that had previously shrouded the room and indicated their being cut off from the human world, Dooks heard a sound he recognized: the gentle pattering of water on the roof of the building.

"It's raining," he said aloud, and hurried off to the window to see for himself.

"Don't!" Manface said behind him, its voice muffled by a mouthful of meat.

Dooks knew the demon was warning him to be careful about being sighted, but the admonition came too late; Dooks was too eager to confirm that he was 'back home' and had already parted the curtains for a look.

It was impossible to describe his relief when he saw that the world as he knew it was back in place again. He almost broke down in tears.

The rain was coming down lightly. The ten or so yards of concrete expanse across to the middle block of rooms shimmered with wetness, but the water had no depth to it, just little pools where the ground was uneven.

The night was wet and peaceful. Dooks thought he'd never seen anything so beautiful.

Dooks looked up over the short hedge lining the rear of the middle block to its windows. The window directly opposite him was shuttered. Dooks looked along the hedge at the others. Three windows down he stopped and gasped. Looking almost as if she'd been hung on the wall, a young woman of unusual beauty was framed in that back window, outlined in the room's soft light. Judging from this distance, she seemed to be in her late twenties and was wearing goth makeup.

Dooks did a mental calculations. If the design of Hicks's room followed the general pattern for the rest of the motel, then the woman was looking out of the bathroom window in her suite. Once more he was struck by how exceptionally beautiful she was, with flawless skin, long black hair and a perfect profile. It was however a bathroom window, smaller and also higher than a regular window so as to prevent the viewing (or the exhibitionism) of those bathing, and so all that was visible to Dooks (at this distance and angle of view) were the girl's head and her shoulders, which were covered in black—looked like a tee shirt with a silver curve on it.

The drizzle was nature's curtain separating them. The pale reflection of the moon in the wet lot made the setting romantic to Dooks.

The woman raised something for a moment, a flash of black and red. Though the black object in her hand clearly looked like a bloody knife, Dooks told himself not to be silly—*Take it easy, man, or soon you'll be projecting your guilt on everyone else.*

Dooks pulled the curtains closer together. If he could see her, she could likewise see him; but she wasn't looking in his direction. She had a preoccupied look on her face, and yes, she also seemed to be talking to herself; muttering something under her breath, her lovely lips parting as if cussing. Either that, or she was talking at very low volume to someone else in the room.

And why am I staring at her anyway? Yes, she's beautiful, but the world is full of beautiful women. And she's clearly there with her boyfriend. It'd be hard for a lady that pretty to be single.

But behind him Manface was still chomping away at Robby's heart. Dooks looked back and almost vomited. Even with its now elongated neck, the creature was having trouble eating the heart, which kept slipping back and forth across the coffee table, sliding about because Manface seemingly couldn't extend the paws of its frozen doggy forelimbs to hold it in place. Most of the coffee table, including the Necromantica spellbook and the evil coin with which the Devil's Coin Game had been played, was smeared with trails of spilled heart-blood and yellow demon saliva. The only conceivable way to speed up the demon's feeding would be for Dooks to hold the half-consumed heart in place for it, something he definitely wasn't about to do; the demon would have to get through its meal on its own.

It's still just 2 a.m. More than enough time for it to do so.

So he kept watching the girl in the third room across from him. He felt slightly guilty spying on her like this, but she wasn't naked, so in reality no harm was being done, and in addition she was very nice to look at indeed.

But then, all of a sudden, the young beauty jerked back out of sight. No, she'd *ducked* out of sight. And next, she pulled the drapes shut. Dooks hadn't imagined her alarm; after her black hair vanished from sight below the sill, he saw a pale hand with glittering fingernails reach up and yank the curtain shut. The action had a curious desperation to it.

That's odd; it's like she's scared of something, Dooks thought. And then he spotted the other woman.

This new woman was walking in the rain, walking close to the hedge by the middle block, but coming from its far end, which was out of Dooks's range of vision. She wore a short blue dress and high heels and was stepping along at a leisurely pace, as if enjoying the fall of water on her body. Her figure was great and her gait—she wasn't walking so much as strutting—screamed 'hooker' in Dooks's mind.

He examined her face as she approached the other woman's window. One of the block's exterior lights was shining directly on her and Dooks saw that she wore more makeup than possibly any woman he'd ever known. And now, as he studied her face she turned and looked directly at him.

No, Dooks was certain that she couldn't actually see him. Even if he'd not had the window drapes as close together as he did, the light shining in her face would prevent her from seeing him. And yet, he had the unshakeable conviction that she *could* see him, that even though at this distance he couldn't make out her eyes, that those very same eyes were staring directly into his, were reading his mind, were speaking to his soul.

The woman in blue paused by the other woman's window and stared across the wetness at him, her eyes penetrating the intervening barriers of the rain's now increasing intensity and motel window glass.

In that instant, Dooks felt something terrifying pass between himself and the hooker. And that something was in no way a sexual invitation. Dooks had no idea what it was otherwise, but its violent impact on his mind forced his eyes shut, and he swayed there beside the window.

When a few seconds later, he pulled himself together and looked across at the woman again, she was gone; her place near the third window replaced by the rain sloshing down from the roof.

That was completely inexplicable to Dooks. If the woman in the blue dress had been standing directly opposite him, here at the end of the block, he could have understood her vanishing; he would have assumed she'd slipped around the side of the block to avoid the rain when he'd closed his eyes.

But I only shut them for three seconds at most, not even enough time for her to cross the parking lot and come over here. She wasn't moving . . . she'd paused . . . when my eyes were shut, I didn't hear feet splashing across . . .

Feeling faint again, Dooks looked up and down the middle block for the woman. He was about to open the room's front door to see if perhaps he was mistaken, if perhaps she had crossed to the rear corridor, but decided it would be stupid to do so.

She's not important, he told himself. *There's no point in me exposing myself just to look for her. But what just happened out there? Who was that woman? Is she the one the other girl was scared of?*

"The answer to your last question is yes," Manface said, causing Dooks to immediately pull the drapes fully shut and turn back towards the room.

"What, mutt?" He had no idea if he'd spoken aloud or if the demon had somehow read his mind. He hoped it was the former and not the latter.

Hey, why do I keep calling this creature 'mutt' instead of its real name? I guess in this case it's my compensation mechanism. It helps my sanity to simplify it to something familiar; after all it really is just a mutt with a human face.

Brownie had been a mongrel and so 'mutt' was an accurate description; as well as a fond term that Dooks had often used for the dog.

Which now raised another question in Dooks's mind:

Hey, is Brownie still in there somewhere, maybe waiting to reappear when this is all over? Or is the dog long gone? Dooks didn't like thinking it was the latter. He hoped it was the former, that when this was all done with, the dog would still be okay. After all, the ritual in the Necromantica spellbook had said nothing about killing the dog; all he and Robby had expected to do was feed it.

So, yeah, maybe calling this thing 'mutt' is my subconscious way of expressing that hope that Brownie's still in there somewhere. It's also comforting and reassuring that Manface doesn't appear to care how I address it.

"What were you saying, mutt?" he repeated, returning his focus to the matter at hand.

"I was replying you," the demon replied, an answer that provided no answer to Dooks's query as to whether or not he'd spoken aloud. "The witch in the other window was frightened of Christine and avoided looking at her. You unfortunately did not."

"Christine? That's the name of that over-made-up hooker just now? So what about her?"

"That was Christine Valona. The problem with her is that she's dead."

Dooks relaxed a bit at that bit of nonsense information. "Dead? Mutt, she looked extremely alive to me. Creepy, but alive."

"Harry, she looks creepy *because* she's dead. Christine Valona is a ghost. She's extremely bad karma for anyone she comes in contact with. I knew she was out there tonight. I tried to warn you not to look out of the window. But you were too stubborn and I was too hungry. Seeing her has terrible consequences for you, I'm afraid."

"A *ghost?* Warn me about . . . ?" Dooks did recall the demon cautioning him, But then, he forgot about finishing the question. With a thrill of elation he realized that Manface had just finished eating Robby's heart. In between telling him that B.S. that the woman in the blue dress was supposedly a ghost, Manface had just snapped up the last piece of heart.

Yeah, the coffee table is a complete disaster now, but the deed is done, and I'm about to become a frigging billionaire . . . Oh, and . . .

And Manface was changing again. Its elongated dog neck was shrinking back to its previous length and its face too was changing.

O-o-o-kay, I guess I should have expected this to happen when I fed it Robby's heart.

Maybe at a subconscious level Dooks *had* expected it to happen. But nonetheless, he still felt very shocked when suddenly the demon now had Robby Mayfield's face.

He looked down at Robby's corpse. Robby no longer had a face, just a completely featureless expanse of skin at the front of his head.

Just like . . .

Dooks spun around to look at Hicks. Hicks, who now seemed in competition with Robby as to which of them was the more gruesome, blood-splattered and messy stiff, was still faceless; which made Dooks look back at Manface again and study the creature's head.

But no, it only had Robby's face; there wasn't another face at the back of its head. *So where'd Hicks's face go? Or is it hidden beneath Robby's?*

CHAPTER 10

Roman

Roman woke up.

After some dillydallying in bed, he realized why he'd woken up. All the beer he'd earlier drank was making its presence felt in his bladder; he desperately needed to pee.

He got out of bed, staggered into the bathroom, and relieved himself.

Then, while washing his hands, his blue eyes traced the writing on the mirror over the washbasin.

'YOU'VE AN APPOINTMENT WITH THE DIVA OF HELL. GET READY AND DON'T BE LATE,' the message read in dripping red letters.

Roman stepped back from the washbasin and blinked his eyes at the mirror. No, he wasn't imagining it. Someone really had written something on the mirror.

Is that blood on the mirror? Who did it? Was it Christine? Recalling her name fetched to his mind a pleasant memory of the great sex they'd had, sex only rivaled by that with his runaway ex Amy. But he also had a memory of the prostitute's face. Just like her excessive use of cosmetics had disguised her real appearance, she had similarly been concealing something from him; that much was certain.

But had she written this on the mirror?

She had to have. After we fucked, Christine used the bathroom. She most likely wrote this as a joke to me. Diva of hell? That's a good one; it's likely a reminder to me to call her.

In his surprise on noticing the writing, Roman had left the sink tap running. Now he stepped back up to the washbasin, rinsed his hands clean and turned off the water. That done, he unrolled some tissue paper from the holder and turned back to wipe off the message on the mirror.

But now, to his surprise, there was nothing written there. The mirror was clean. This made Roman step back from the washbasin again. He stood there, blinking his eyes and wondering what was happening.

Courtesy of all the beer, he now had a slight headache. It didn't take him much to decide his mind was playing tricks on him.

But when he walked out of the bathroom, he saw that the door to his motel room was wide open. It was raining heavily outside and the wind had blown some rain into the room; the rug just past the threshold was wet. The door itself swung lightly to and fro in a gentle arc.

I thought Christine shut the door when she left, Roman thought. On his left the TV was showing a late-night political interview.

Roman started across to shut the door, but then a dual sweep of headlights cut through the downpour, making him remember he was butt naked and the light in his motel room was on. He leapt back out of sight just as a brown SUV rolled past, and then picked up his shorts from the floor by the bed. After pulling them on, he once more walked over to the door.

Arriving at the door, he decided against closing it immediately. Instead, he stood there, watching the rain and the wall of trees opposite through which he had glimpses of Carver Street and the buildings across the road. A van rolled loudly past, its headlights piercing the rain. The brown SUV that had earlier startled him had parked at the far end of the block to his right, and an elderly couple were getting out of it, both fumbling with umbrellas because of the downpour. The man and woman finally escaped the rain and entered their room, and the night resumed its noisy silence.

Roman watched the rain for a while longer. Several times the wind was almost directly in his face; blowing water over his bare feet, but it didn't bother him.

By his watch the time was 2:15 a.m.

I wasn't asleep for long, but what with imagining that writing on the bathroom mirror and Christine leaving the door open, I'm not gonna fall asleep again any time soon. Guess I'll just have another beer and watch some TV.

But this wasn't to be. As Roman was stepping back into the room he heard footsteps approaching along the front block's external corridor.

"Hey, Roman! Hold on, Roman."

His first thought—that Christine had either returned for something she'd forgotten, or simply needed to use his bathroom again—was quickly nixed, because the voice calling him was male and very low-pitched.

"Hey, Roman! Wait!"

Roman had already stepped back into the room and had his hand on the edge of the door, ready to push it shut, but the fact that this unseen person knew his name made him pause. Assuming it was most likely the guy at the reception desk who wanted him for something, he stepped forward again.

It wasn't the guy at the reception desk. A muscular man with completely red skin and wearing just shorts was heading for him.

Roman needed no further encouragement to shut the door. He leapt back into the room, slammed the door, and quickly slipped the chain on.

Then he stood there, one hand on the door, one hand on the wall, breathing hard and trembling. He heard the rush of footsteps reach the door and cease. Next, through the wood he heard a sigh of frustration.

Who the hell is that freak? For fuck's sake, I need a beer!

Roman turned from the door to get his beer and almost screamed. The red man was now sitting on his couch. His entire body was as crimson as red paint . . . or freshly spilled blood. His shorts were made of black leather.

"You could simply have let me in," the man said in his deep voice, and that was when Roman first noticed the pair of short, slightly curved black horns—like a goat or ram might have—on the man's head, which was either naturally bald or freshly shaven. He sneaked a look at the man's hands and his bare feet. Other than for black fingernails and toenails all four extremities looked human enough.

But his head . . . those two horns jutting from his temples looked like they'd grown there naturally.

"Who are you?" Roman asked in a timid voice, regretting that after hurrying inside the motel room he'd taken the time to put the chain on the door. *Otherwise I could just yank the door open and run off into the night. No, that won't work. I locked the door to get away from him and yet he's in here with me!*

"My name is Breakwind," the man replied.

"Wha-wha-what are y-y-you?" Roman stammered.

"I'm a demon," the red-skinned man replied. "I've come from hell to escort you to your appointment with the Diva."

"Huh?"

Breakwind pointed to the bathroom. "I left a message on your mirror. When the message vanished I knew you'd woken up and read it and so I'm here to collect you."

"I see," Roman said. But really he didn't see, and was in fact wondering if maybe Christine had slipped him some LSD while they had sex, or maybe earlier when they'd been drinking before having sex. *But no, she had only the one beer and I was the one who handed it to her. And in addition, Christine never once left my sight, except for when she went to use the bathroom.*

So, no, he hadn't taken LSD and as such couldn't be hallucinating. *There really is a horned demon sitting in my motel room. And, so yeah, I really did see that writing on the mirror earlier.*

"You ready to go?" Breakwind asked.

"Do I have a choice?" Roman asked in return.

"Not really. If you don't come willingly I've instructions to knock you out and carry you to Diva's residence. She insists it's essential she sees you tonight and my job is to obey her orders." As if to make his point, the demon flexed his left arm—he had impressive biceps.

Roman nodded. "No need to get violent. I'll come along willing. But first I need a fucking beer." He strode past Breakwind and got one from the six-pack in the fridge. "You want one too?" he offered the demon.

"Thank you." The demon accepted the can and opened it, licking his lips in anticipation. Twenty seconds later the can was empty and crushed on the coffee table and the demon grinned, showing long and sharp black teeth.

"Yeah, that really hit the spot," he said. "You hardly ever get grade-A beer in hell." He stared across at Roman with eyes that held a threat in them. "Hey, dude, it's time to go."

Roman had only taken two gulps of his own beer, but he put the can down. "Yeah, sure. Hold on a sec, let me put some more clothes on."

But Breakwind was already getting to his feet. "No need to. You're okay wearing just your shorts like that. Hell is very warm and if you're overdressed you'll just wind up sweating a lot. And besides, we're headed to hell's Sex Realm, where Diva rules. Chances are, once there, even your shorts won't remain on you for very long." Breakwind gestured over the couch, at the pair of blue flip-flops near the bed. Just put those on, so you don't bruise or burn your feet."

Roman gulped. "Okay." He stepped across the room, and put on his slippers, and then, on an impulse, picked up his cellphone.

"Dude, who're you planning to call from hell?" Breakwind asked.

Roman put the cellphone back on the nightstand. The way he viewed it, since he knew he wasn't hallucinating, he was either mad or . . .

"Just imagine you're dreaming," Breakwind told him as he stepped towards the door. "It's easier at first if you think you'll wake up later."

Roman nodded and followed the demon out of the room.

***

Outside the rain was still falling hard.

The water splashing off the hood of Roman's car and sprayed over both himself and his companion.

"This way," Breakwind said, turning left towards the reception building.

Roman walked alongside the red-skinned demon. In this combination of whistling wet weather and night there was no one about, no one outside to see him; and yet he felt very conspicuous wearing just his shorts.

The deserted state of the motel however didn't last very long. By the time Roman had taken six steps forward beside Breakwind the parking lot was full of people.

Roman tried to understand what had just happened. A moment ago the Sunflower Motel had been dark and assaulted by liquid nature, mostly lit by whichever shifting eye of moon managed to peek through the storm clouds; and there had been half a dozen cars in the parking lot . . . And now . . . all the motel's lights were on, the parking lot was completely empty of vehicles, and there were people everywhere; joking, laughing, carousing; and entering and exiting motel rooms, in most cases with their arms wrapped around each other.

Stranger yet, the majority of the mob that now filled the motel parking lot were either barely clothed or not clothed at all.

Roman rubbed his eyes with the heels of his hands, but afterwards had to admit that he wasn't seeing things.

"Welcome to hell," Breakwind said.

"This is hell? It looks more like a Mardi Gras party." He paid closer attention to the mob, and was now able to separate them into two categories. Roughly half of them, both men and women (or rather male and female, as some of the 'men' and 'women' looked rather odd, and didn't fit into any of the normal binary and queer gender categories) had the same red skin as his companion; while the other fifty percent were clearly human, with a roughly even racial distribution.

A good number of the red-skinned people had horns and/or tails of different shapes and lengths and sizes. A few of them even had wings.

Yes, they're demons. So, unless I'm dreaming, this is most definitely hell. And when did it stop raining?

Roman put his not immediately noticing the difference in the weather down to his confusion at he and Breakwind's sudden and seamless transition to this place. Here the floor was dry; smooth but rough as his flip-flops informed his feet. In addition to this lack of moisture, the air was noticeably warm; which might explain the general lack of clothing here. In fact the air was so warm that Roman understood why Breakwind had told him not to get dressed before accompanying him.

Looking up, there were neither moon nor clouds overhead, just a glowing red ceiling that seemed a mile away.

Except for its current state of human/demon activity the motel looked exactly the same. So did the wide expanse of parking lot. The one immediately noticeable difference in the layout of this place was that there no longer existed a wall of trees opposite the front block, or any road either. Here the trees had been replaced by a wall of dark reddish rock that was penetrated by nooks, alcoves, and arched doorways, at the mouths of which couples frolicked sexually. In the wide chamber accessed through one arched doorway, an orgy was taken place; with people doing just about everything imaginable to each other.

Roman watched men and women and demons sucking penises; men, women and demons licking vaginas; men and women and demons fisting and fucking and sodomizing one another.

"Everyone here seems to be having a great time," Roman said as he and Breakwind both stepped out of the way of an approaching couple: a very tall demoness leading along a fat man on hands and knees like a poodle. "I thought hell was where one went to be tormented for all eternity."

They paused to watch the dominant/submissive pair. The kinky couple passed them, with the submissive barking and shaking his behind like he was actually a dog.

Breakwind laughed at the departing pair and then told Roman, "This is one of the surface regions of hell; the torment of the eternally damned occurs in hell's lower regions. Simply put: the lower you go, the hotter it becomes."

Roman nodded. His ears made out soft snatches of erotic, seductive, and rhythmic music, and the much louder panting, moaning, gasping, and groaning of those participating in the sexual activities.

"This Sex Realm is a realm of never-ending erotic enjoyment." Breakwind continued. "No one here does anything but fuck, and the Diva reigns supreme over them all."

Roman's attempt to ask a further question about their surroundings was cut short by another approaching group of people. In this case a seventyish woman in a wheelchair, flanked by two demons and a human man, who were joking with her as they pushed her chair along. Of course, under any normal conditions there would be nothing wrong with this scenario; her three male companions could be her sons. But in this case both the old woman and her three companions were naked. In addition to this, all three males—human and demon alike—sported monstrous erections, two of which the old lady gripped firmly in her withered hands and stroked and manipulated, sliding both heavy foreskins back and forth.

Both of the demons accompanying the woman nodded greetings to Breakwind as they passed. As they went by, Roman estimated that both of their penises were at least a foot-and-a-half long and as thick around as his wrist. Even the human member of their trio was ridiculously, almost surgically, well hung.

"Oh yeah, baby, I've really been looking forward to this," the old lady said excitedly, though in a weak, exhausted-sounding voice.

"Aw, come on, dude," Roman whispered to Breakwind in horrified fascination. "Surely that old girl in the wheelchair isn't gonna . . . "

"Yes, Mrs. Roosevelt is going to have sex with them. All three of them."

"But . . . but . . ." The size of the two demonic erections horrified him. "How the hell does she expect to survive it? Those dicks are so large they'll tear her apart."

"She doesn't expect to survive it," Breakwind informed him in an amused voice. Mrs. Roosevelt is dying of cancer. Being fucked to death by men with giant penises is the single item left unchecked on her bucket list. She came here to die in ecstasy and that is exactly what will happen to her."

Roman watched Mrs. Roosevelt and her naked companions cross the parking lot towards one of the arched doorways.

And why am I still calling it a parking lot? There are no cars down here. Of course, he understood that he was being subjective by assuming they were 'down here.' But then every religion he knew held that hell was underground.

"Hey, come on, we're wasting time," Breakwind told Roman, taking hold of his wrist and pulling him along the walkway. "I do understand that this is all new to you and as such very stare-worthy, but the Diva don't like to be kept waiting. In addition, she already impressed on me the importance of getting you to her ASAP."

"I don't see what the hurry is," Roman said while allowing the demon to drag him along.

"Well, neither do I, but then the lady is the boss."

He steered Roman past a couple who were having sex on the corridor. Roman watched them in amusement for a moment and then was confused, because he couldn't tell if it was the man or the woman who had an erection and was penetrating the other or if both of them did and were.

This just gets weirder and weirder and weirder, he thought as they left the end of the block behind them and crossed what back on Earth(?) had been the grassy lawn that separated the front block from the reception building.

Here however, there was no grass, just bare red rock on which an orgy was happening: about a dozen human and demon bodies writhing on the ground and pleasuring themselves in every way imaginable, and also in a few ways that made Roman blink because he didn't think they were possible.

With all of this happening around him, Roman wasn't surprised to discover he once more had an erection. But seeing as (except for Breakwind) all the males here were similarly erect, his own state of sexual excitement paled into insignificance; his hardened penis was merely a minor unit in a major whole, that whole seemingly being the sexual fervor that consumed all those here.

Careful not to interrupt any penetrations, orgasms, or male/female ejaculations, they stepped over and through the carpet of entwined lovers.

During this brief interlude when Breakwind wasn't dragging him along, Roman got a proper look at his new surroundings.

Beyond the orgiastic revelers strewn out on the ground, both the middle and rear blocks of the motel existed as he remembered them from Earth. The sex party extended over there too and seemingly far and wide beyond the motel. This was truly the Sex Realm. Sex without an end.

Roman couldn't understand where all these people came from; how they had all arrived here. *Or are they like me: brought here on this Diva person's instructions?*

But as he and Breakwind approached the reception building, an exciting thought occurred to him: *Is Diva actually Amy?* He felt a rush of intense emotions at this possibility; at the suggestion that he might soon be face-to-face again with the woman he'd loved above all others and whom he still carried a candle for.

But then he scolded himself: *Don't be a moron, man. What the hell would Amy, of all people, be doing here?*

Amy had been simply the cute girl next door. Of course she had enjoyed sex; she was healthy and normal. But Amy had liked her sex in every shade of vanilla, very simple and very sweet and tender, not . . . He winced as he watched someone shove their fist up somebody else's welcoming vagina. *Oh no, Amy isn't here, except she's being held captive by someone. One look at this place and she'd run off screaming.*

They had now navigated their way through the tangle of copulating bodies.

"Well, here we are," Breakwind said, gesturing towards the steps that entered the reception building.

Roman studied the sign over the building. "Yeah, it figures," he said on seeing that this sex establishment was called the 'ORGASM MOTEL.'

CHAPTER 11

Mandy & Tenebra

"And so now I'm off to hell," Tenebra informed Mandy with a cold smile on her face.

Mandy Cherry would have loved to point out to Tenebra that she'd already told her as much, but she was currently in no condition to do so.

She'd revived again five minutes ago to find herself once more tied up on the motel room couch. And this time she'd also been gagged. Since then she'd been fighting through a combination of her new headache and her worries.

From outside came the soft patter of rain; Mandy didn't know how long she'd been out for. But the air smelt clean and she could hear a rumble of distant thunder as if there had been a storm during her unconsciousness that had worn itself out now.

Mandy, who'd awoken lying flat on her back with her captor frowning down at her, had already attempted to free her wrists again, but had quickly realized that there was no chance of her doing so. Where previously she'd been able to grab hold of a loose end of cord, now both those loose ends were secured around her neck.

Tenebra had meanwhile discarded both her thong and her black tee shirt. Doing so had revealed the black and red pentagram painted on her belly. The ugly 'head' amulet dangled between her naked breasts.

Tenebra had already told Mandy the reason for her nakedness. "I'm off to hell's *Sex Realm*—for obvious reasons, hardly anyone ever wears clothes there."

Mandy had nodded that she understood, but her mind hadn't been on what Tenebra was saying, because at that very moment her eyes had just focused on what lay behind Tenebra, which was of course, Dewdrop. Of course Mandy knew her dead girlfriend's corpse was over there, but because Tenebra had been standing in the way since she'd revived from her unconsciousness, she had had no idea that anything had changed about the corpse.

But something had. A little detail, but disturbing nonetheless:

Now there was a large black candle sticking out of Dewdrop's body—one of those from Tenebra's box of witchcraft goodies on the coffee table. The candle was stuck into the hole in Dewdrop's body that had killed her. She was lying on her belly and the candle, which was unlit, protruded from the lower left side of her back. Above it, between Dewdrop's shoulder blades, was painted a black pentagram that Mandy knew hadn't been there earlier.

The sight chilled Mandy deeply. It also made her look around for the zombie woman. But although Kelli's head still lay at the same place by the wall, her reanimated body was not to be seen; meaning she was on the other side of the room.

Mandy realized she'd run out of options. *Damn, except this witch makes a mistake, I'll be dead soon. And with this gag in my mouth, I can't talk now to distract her into making that mistake.*

She winced when Tenebra picked up her long black knife from the couch near her feet. Her ankles weren't tied together and she wondered why. She didn't think it was because Tenebra had again overlooked the possibility of Mandy kicking her.

Her mind leapt to her second meeting with the prostitute Christine Valona, whom she now knew really was dead. She cursed the ghost deep down in her soul. *If that bitch Christine hadn't messed up my escape, I'd be well gone from here now!*

She regarded Tenebra with hatred. *Oh no, witch, my death isn't kismet! I refuse to die without putting up a fight!*

Tenebra in turn, regarded her with a speculative look in her eyes and then said, "Okay, I'd better warn before we start that this is gonna hurt like hell. Unfortunately for you, you're not dead like your girlfriend. And also, where you're concerned, my preparations need to be more intricate." She laughed sadistically. "You can scream all you like behind that gag!"

Mandy knew that something horrible was about happening to her; her state of apprehension was almost a welcome distraction.

Tenebra picked up something from the coffee table.

No, no, no! Mandy thought when she saw Tenebra was holding a red candle, though one smaller than that which she'd stuck in Dewdrop.

Oh my God, no! Mandy shrieked in her mind, when Tenebra, who was now licking her lips, bent over her and stabbed her in the left breast with the knife. The pain was horrible. Mandy barely managed not to wet herself. She gaped in disbelief at her chest, at the bleeding hole Tenebra was making above her left nipple, and then she blacked out to the sound of Tenebra's chanting.

When she revived, she saw that the deed was done. Implanted by brutality, and seemingly held in place by her own clotted blood, the red candle stuck firmly out of her breast.

She gaped at Tenebra in horror. Tenebra, licked her black-glossed lips again and winked back at her. "One down, only three left to go!"

Three more? Are you fucking nuts!? She wished she wasn't gagged and could give proper vent to her terror, her rage and her agony, because Tenebra was already stabbing into her right breast too. Blood squirted out and hit the witch in the face; she licked it off her lips, grinned evilly, and kept up the bad work.

Once more, Mandy passed out and awakened to find a candle implanted in her breast. Both of her breasts were slicked with blood now; which made her question how the candles stuck in them weren't being shifted and ejected by her heavy breathing. The answer seemed obvious though—magic. Her tormented breasts felt strangely full and solid, almost as if their fat content had fallen in love with the invading candlewax and gotten married to it.

"That's a cool trick you've got—fainting like that," Tenebra told her. "You'll need to do it at least one more time."

Mandy, who was now blinking back tears, assumed Tenebra intended to cut into her vagina next. *She's headed for some fucking sex realm, isn't she? And so far she's attacked my breasts, so my pussy will definitely be her next point of call, and the pervy bitch is saving my asshole for la—Shiiit!"*

She screamed into the gag again and looked down at herself in bewilderment. The pain had come from her midriff, and it took her a few seconds to understand why: the evil witch had stabbed her in the navel. Indeed, this fresh brutality hurt Mandy more than the previous two had, because Tenebra was taking her time with it. Almost like she was performing a circumcision, she was slicing around the navel, excising it from Mandy's body. Tenebra's hands were slick with blood, and the already excised semicircle of navel flesh kept slipping from her grasp as she worked with a manic smile on her face.

This time Mandy really passed out. Tenebra's guttural chanting was the last thing she heard as she slipped away into a welcome darkness.

***

When Mandy next awoke, the world looked different to her. At first she thought her pain had driven her crazy, but then she realized that she'd been turned upside down while she was unconscious. Her head and shoulders were down on the bloody rug by the couch and her legs were up in the air, held in position by headless zombie Terri.

Oh fuck! Mandy thought as pain coursed through her belly, and then she understood why. The black candle that stuck out of her navel must have been a foot long, and this was just the exposed portion of it. It was about three inches in diameter and as far as she could tell from how much pain she was experiencing, seemed to have been forced all the way through her body and glued directly onto her spinal column. Tenebra had even wiped the blood away and drawn a black pentagram around the candle.

Mandy really hurt now. She twisted herself, trying to alter her position to reduce the pain, but motion hurt even more than remaining still did, so she hung there upside down, staring up at headless Terri who held her ankles in place.

Where the hell is the madwoman who did this to me? Where is she? I'll kill her for this! Then she froze in fear. *There's still one more to come! What horror is next? Is she gonna drill a hole in my head and stick a candle in my brains too? Why am I upside down with my damn legs in the air?*

She felt terrified, but also curious. Then she realized all hope wasn't yet lost: *Tenebra left her knife on the coffee table. If I can just reach it, I can cut myself free again.*

The long black knife lay with its tip dripping blood onto the already bloody rug. Mandy pondered how to reach it:

First of all, I need to get myself back upright again and then—

Her fresh escape plans died for the moment when Tenebra walked back into view.

"Hi, down there, glad you're awake now. How do you feel?"

Mandy glared impotent hatred up at her. *You just wait till I get out of these bonds again! This time I won't make the same mistake I did last time. This time I won't leave here until you're dead! I'll hack off your head just like we did Kelli's!*

101

"There's no point blaming me for what's happening to you now," Tenebra said mockingly, after squatting and tapping the tip of Mandy's nose with her index finger. "If you really desire to apportion blame for your current unfortunate situation, blame Petra Velli for sending you two to murder me. Actually, blame yourselves for considering my life to be worth a measly two hundred grand. Personally I'd value it at about a hundred million." She smiled. "But then, thanks so much for coming here tonight. See, I needed three fresh corpses to perform this ritual to open the door into hell's Sex Realm, and not being a particularly bloodthirsty witch, I've never had them." She laughed. "Or maybe, that should rather be, that I didn't have anyone I'd happily sacrifice without qualms; and whom no one would miss afterwards. And if you two"—she gestured over at Dewdrop—"had just left here after killing Kelli, I'd have let you go too—you'd have been a great alibi to Petra that I was dead and gone."

She flicked the unlit candle sticking from Mandy's right breast, making her tremble with agony. "But since you didn't go when the going was good—well, here we are now. You get to die and go to hell. While, I . . . I also get to go to hell, but *alive* and to the fun part of the place." Tenebra leered and stroked her bare crotch and ground it against her hand while making thrusting motions. "I can assure you, girl, that the only hellfire *I'll* be feeling is the one between my thighs."

Then she sighed. "But let's not waste any more time. I'm sure you're impatient to die, while I'm impatient to finish this."

Mandy cringed at the statement. That meant it was time to get cut again.

But no, Tenebra grinned down at her. "Don't be afraid. The good part for you is that I'm not about cutting you again. While the bad part is . . . I'm about to shit in your vajayjay!"

What!? Mandy caught her breath. *What!?*

Outside the rain had just stopped as if it too couldn't believe its ears; and that lack of noise seemed the perfect space for Mandy to make sense of what she'd just heard. But she couldn't make sense of what Tenebra had just said: *Did she really just say she's gonna SHIT in my PUSSY?*

"Oh yes, Mandy, you heard me right," Tenebra said. She was laughing, clearly unable to contain her amusement at her victim's wide-eyed shock. "I'm going to take a crap in your vagina. It's the last requirement of my ritual."

Tenebra said something to Kelli, who now parted Mandy's legs. Mandy tried to resist being spread open like this, but the headless woman's grip was irresistible; the muscle and bone of Mandy's thighs couldn't negotiate with fingers as rigid as steel.

"Yeah, like that," Tenebra said, directing traffic. "Bend her knees too, so I can get between her thighs."

Mandy suddenly understood that Tenebra was arranging her in a porn pose. She had seen similar poses in hardcore girl-on-girl videos, when the lesbians were attempting either an advanced form of scissoring, or athletic strap-on sex. She had even once suggested to Dewdrop that they try it out, but Dewdrop had been stoned at the time, had burst out laughing, and next had fallen asleep. Mandy had herself been so amused by Dewdrop's stoned response that she hadn't ever repeated the request; each time she was going to, she'd remember Dewdrop snoring that night with her buttocks up in the air, and instead burst out laughing.

But now, Mandy herself was similarly positioned, shoulders and head on the floor, waist up in the air, propped in place by her back against the couch.

No, no, no! she thought in dread. She tried twisting away as Tenebrae began caressing her thighs, but her tormentor merely flipped the candle stuck into her belly and her resistance ended in a burst of nerve-racking anguish.

"Oh, what a pretty pussy you have," Tenebra said as Mandy felt her fingers first stroking it, then penetrating it and then stretching the soft entrance to her body seemingly as wide open as the bathroom door.

She began weeping.

With one foot up on the couch and her other foot on the floor, Tenebra positioned herself between Mandy's legs as if they were about scissoring and then . . .

Mandy couldn't watch herself anymore. She looked away and then shut her eyes. But she could still feel what was being done to her.

Despite the trio of universes of pain that were tearing up her breasts and her belly, she felt with unanimous lack of debate that having another woman defecate inside her vagina was the worst experience she had ever had. And Tenebra seemed to be constipated; in addition to seeming never-ending in length, the horrible piece of shit, the evil turd that was penetrating her sex, felt as fat and as hard and painful as being fisted without sufficient lube or being sodomized with an overlarge dildo. She felt ultimately degraded. She would gladly have died to escape living through this.

Finally it was over. Her vagina felt packed full to overflowing. Looking up again as Tenebra got off of her, Mandy imagined the brown end of the turd poking out between her defiled labia.

Her humiliation was complete. She'd just been used as a human toilet, rendered of no consequence by another woman. She wondered how Tenebra could be so *evil*. She felt it would have been more acceptable if a member of the evil patriarchy had done this to her. Mandy knew that at heart men were nasty and evil creatures; one expected behavior like this from them. A woman didn't expect to be treated this way by another woman, someone similarly oppressed by the opposite sex.

Her tears were flowing freely now, streaming sideways off her face onto the rug.

Tenebra laughed at her tears. "Don't worry, I won't tell anyone else how I just packed your pretty pussy full of poop. And now, to prevent it from slipping out . . ."

Mandy's eyes widened in additional shock and agony as Tenebra forced a fat black candle down into her vagina on top of the excrement. "There, now you're all nicely plugged up."

With a witchy cackle, Tenebra fetched a cigarette lighter from the box on the coffee table and began lighting the candles stuck into Mandy's body.

Suddenly, Mandy Cherry was unable to endure any more of this degradation. Her mind began cracking up. Slowly, what could be considered 'herself' fragmented and went into freefall, with quadrants of her personality splitting off and sailing away into space, seeking freedom from the horrible things that were happening to her.

CHAPTER 12

Dooks

The evil coin had reverted to normal. What now lay on the bloody coffee table was just a regular quarter.

Finally, Dooks thought. *That's a relief. As long as it had the devil's face on it, I couldn't help thinking the game was about to continue.*

Harry Dooks felt sweaty with anticipation now that the important moment had arrived. He felt too excited to remain upright, and so sat in his previous armchair facing Manface.

"Okay, and now I get to make my wish," he informed the demon in a gloating voice. Seeing as the demon currently had Robby's face the gloating came naturally; it felt like he was rubbing Robby's defeat in his face again. But really, he knew Robby was long gone; a glance at his faceless corpse more than confirmed that.

"Yes, it's time to make your *single* wish," Manface agreed. "I have to remind you of that."

Dooks waved the demon's words away. "Don't bother, I know I've got only one wish and I know exactly what I'm wishing for. Listen, mutt, I want—"

"Not so fast, Harry," Manface interrupted him.

Dooks scowled at the human-faced dog statue. "What the hell is the matter now?"

Manface smiled a parody of Robby's usual drunken leer. "Well, at the moment there's a slight complication."

"What fucking complication? You aren't trying to screw me out of my one wish too, are you?"

"No, no, no. Nothing like that. Just hear me out while I explain to you the bad implications of your seeing that dead woman Christine Valona earlier."

"Go on, I'm listening."

Manface explained and Dooks listened: "To avoid spending all eternity roasting in hell herself, Christine Valona made a deal with the devil. She agreed to collect six hundred and sixty-six souls for him; in return for which she gets to become a succubus. It works like this— you see Christine and you're screwed; she's one up on her soul-collection tally, and you're on a one-way trip to a bed beneath a tombstone. Of course, some people do go to heaven instead, which upsets her calculations—so, her killing you doesn't automatically guarantee you'll wind up in hell, but I'm sure you get the picture I'm painting here. Dead means dead however you look at it.

"And that's why, Harry," Manface finished, "my honest suggestion to you now is that you make your single wish one for a long life."

Dooks just stared at the demon; he felt flabbergasted. "What? You're telling me not to wish for a billion dollars like I intend to?"

The demon seemed to be trying to nod; its lack of head motion made this impossible, but the skin on its chin jiggled annoyingly. "That is exactly what I mean. Weren't you paying attention just now? At the moment your life is completely forfeit. No matter what you attempt, you've no chance in hell—and I should know, I'm a demon—no chance at all of leaving this motel alive tonight."

Dooks shook his head. "This is impossible. I don't believe you. All I have to do is walk around the end of this block and I'm outa here."

"Trust me, Harry, you won't even make it to the end of the block."

Dooks scowled at Manface. "Trust you? Why the hell should I trust you? You're a demon! We both know you guys lie for fun."

This time Dooks had the sense that had Manface been capable of doing so, it would have shrugged the dog's frozen shoulders. "Okay, guilty as charged—we infernals do lie all the time; it's our stock in trade. But, Harry, I happen to like you. The way you cheated Robby out of his win totally endeared you to me. And so, I'm making this exception and being honest with you. For tonight at least, you need to forget about making any wish for money. Just wish to live for a good long time. Wish for anything else and you're dead meat. Just think, what use is money if you can't spend it?"

"I need to think about this," Dooks said.

"Take your time, I'm not going anywhere yet."

Dooks shut his eyes and thought. *This is totally insane—like Fate is trying to screw me! I've killed two people tonight and I don't get a cent for it . . . !?*

He opened his eyes and gestured around at the two corpses in the room. "Hey, mutt, what happens to the evidence afterwards? Who cleans it up?"

"Don't worry about that. I'll take the bodies to hell with me. There'll be no proof you were here. Have you made up your mind yet?"

"Not yet." Dooks shut his eyes again. *Okay, so that's taken care of. I can do like the demon says, walk away alive and chalk tonight down as a really weird experience . . . But what if the demon is lying? Yeah, what if it is? If I ask it again, it's sure to tell me it's telling me the truth, but is it? How the hell do I know that that woman I saw really was dead? Okay, the other girl—the beauty at the window—her weird behavior seems to indicate that the demon is telling the truth, but what if that girl simply needed to take a quick pee; or someone in the room—her boyfriend or maybe even her pimp—had told her to stop fucking around by the window? That too could've made her react so suddenly. I was too far off to hear what was going on in there. And if that's true, if that's what really happened with her, then I'll have screwed myself out of a billion clams by listening to Manface, who'll then go back to hell and tell the other demons how it just outsmarted another dumb human.*

Such were the sensible thoughts that flittered through Harry Dooks's mind as he sat there with eyes closed and focused on the problem of what to wish for.

Weighing all the possibilities that Manface was lying to him didn't help much, seeing that what hung in the balance here was his survival tonight, his life. *If it is telling me the truth, I had better do what it says—life isn't something that can be replaced, but money can. Bad as things are at the moment, they're certain to improve given time. And in the meanwhile, seeing as Manface says he'll dispose of all the evidence, I can simply go on living at Robby's place. I'll just tell everyone he said he was going on a trip to visit old friends in Jersey City.*

It was tempting. Forget tonight, walk away. Pretend none of this ever happened. But of course take the Necromantica spellbook along with him so he could hold the ritual again in the future—if he dared.

But then something else occurred to Harry Dooks. This was the fact that people in his family tended to live well into old age. His grandfather and grandmother were both still alive, both in their nineties. His mother and father too. As were a whole pantheon of aunts and uncles, and several granduncles and grandaunts too; no one in the Dooks clan seemed to be in the slightest of a hurry to kick the bucket.

And so why should it be any different with me? For all I know, my genes may prove a natural antidote to Christine's so-called curse. But then, if I'm just being stupid I'm so going to reg—

Manface's voice interrupted his thoughts:

"You're taking a hell of a long time making up your mind," the demon said reasonably. "I shouldn't think it'd be that hard. Harry, it's a simple choice: do you want to live, or do you want to die?"

CHAPTER 13

Roman

The interior of the motel reception was empty except for four people. The demoness behind the reception desk was whipping a man chained to an X-frame with her tail, which had to be at least six feet long. Seeing as this was the Sex Realm, her bound partner understandably had an erection.

Across the room from the flagellants, a woman hung on a gallows was masturbating furiously while being raised and lowered on the noose, which turned out to be the looped end of her demon partner's ridiculously long tail, slung up over a ceiling beam for the purpose.

"Yes yes, oh my beloved Satan, yes!" the woman dangling from the noose moaned in delight, instantly putting paid to any suspicion that she was being tortured.

"Come on," Breakwind told Roman, while waving to the red female behind the desk.

"Oh, he's the one the boss wants to see," she replied while lashing her partner across the chest with her tail, the end of which was broken up into seven or eight thin strands.

She leered at Roman, exposing her long black fangs. "Hey, honey, you're cute. I'd love to lash you sometime."

"Not on your life, girl," Roman said nervously, gesturing to the red welts on the demoness' partner's body. The man's torso looked like she had been painting him with red lines. Roman didn't want any of that kinky shit.

"But he likes it, see?" the demoness protested with an amusing pout, reaching out and grabbing the man's penis, which she now manipulated with smooth strokes so that he ejaculated onto her red fingers.

The man gasped and sagged against her, sucking on the pointed tip of her right ear.

"Baby, I'll take a raincheck." Roman nodded politely and he and Breakwind moved on, stepping near the woman on the makeshift gallows, who was now being anally penetrated by her demon partner while she still both asphyxiated on the end of his tail and masturbated energetically. Her face was blue from lack of oxygen and her eyes bulged slightly, but overall her facial expression was one of intense ecstasy. One of her hands was up in the air, wrapped around the tail throttling her, while her other hand divided its actions between plowing her genital furrow and reaching behind her and clamping onto the buttocks of the demon thrusting into her.

Roman and Breakwind walked past her and through a door, into a hallway that ended at a flight of steps.

"Go upstairs," Breakwind indicated. "The Diva is waiting for you."

Roman looked first at the indicated stairs and then back at Breakwind. "You're not coming?"

Breakwind scratched the base of his left horn with a black fingernail. "No, just go upstairs, and walk to the end of the hallway there. You can't miss it. I'll be down here when you're done talking to the Diva." Then he leered and licked his lips. "In the meantime, dude, I'm gonna see about cumming on the receptionist's breasts. Maybe I'll even whip that cute ass of hers with her own tail."

Roman nodded and headed up the stairs.

Climbing them had the aspect of a dream for him; indeed it seemed to him as if he still dreamt. He was well familiar with the kind of dreams that occurred in layers; dreams in which one believed one had woken up, only to find that one was still dreaming, discovering that the previous dream had been the result of one's falling asleep in the current dream.

But if this is a dream, it sure is the granddaddy of them all.

Testing something he had read somewhere, Roman slammed his left forearm hard against the banister. It hurt.

That settles it, he decided. *I'm not dreaming. One supposedly cannot feel pain in a dream.*

Of course, Roman felt scared; this experience beat even that time he'd done acid in uni and wound up thinking his frat brothers were werewolves and the fraternity cat was out to steal his soul. That had been a crazy, surreal experience. But this was crazier than that. Back that time on acid he'd had the reassurance of his friends' voices, though liquid and distorted, slipping in through the cracks in his LSD experience, telling him he was just tripping and that it would wear off in a few hours' time.

But here and now . . . ?

He shook his head as he stepped onto the upper landing.

Were it not that no one here seems to be interested in harming me, I'd have been scared shitless. Of course, all the sex happening around here isn't doing my boner any favors.

His resurgent erection was rampant now. His glans lifted the left hem of his shorts like a sniper aiming at the enemy.

The second floor hallway led to a wide chamber. Roman stepped inside and looked around.

The left side of the chamber was a woman's bedroom, while the right side was her living room. Set off a little to the right of the bedroom area, but not dead center to the hallway, (possibly because of approaching visitors, seeing as her toilet was similarly situated on the opposite side of the room), was her bathing area.

This bathing area was mostly occupied by a large stone claw-footed bathtub. At the moment Diva lounged in the tub, bathing in milk being squeezed from the ten nipples of a multiple-breasted demoness, whose breasts were arranged in pairs from her chest to her crotch.

This copiously lactating demoness was very fat, which Roman agreed was only to be expected considering the amount of milk she had so far squeezed into Diva's bathtub.

Diva was human; a blonde woman with incredibly pale skin. The upper half of her face—her nose and everything above it—was completely obscured by a golden mask which, on closer observation seemed glued onto her head.

"Hello, Roman," she waved on noticing him. Then she dipped a sponge into the milk and held it out to him. "Here, help me do my back."

Roman accepted the sponge from her and knelt behind her.

"I'm sorry I summoned you on such short notice," she said while he washed her back. "But I'm delighted you could make it."

Above them jets of milk still cascaded down from the demoness' many breasts. Like a living showerhead attachment, she was aiming her squirts at Diva, not at the water. Some of the milk splashed on Roman. It was hot, but not uncomfortably so. A squirt or two hit him on the lips. He licked it. It tasted like regular milk.

Diva finally waved a hand at the lactating demoness; the bathtub was by now more than three-quarters filled with milk. "That is enough for now, Mamasi."

"Yes, ma'am." Mamasi bowed and straightened up. The flow of milk from her breasts immediately stopped, with her nipples' final expulsions streaming down her thighs. Roman was impressed by how she could seemingly turn her milk production on and off with a mental command like someone urinating.

Mamasi bowed again and left.

"Would you like to join me in the bathtub?" Diva asked Roman.

Roman did a mental calculation. There was definitely room for two in the bathtub.

"Thanks, but I'll wait," he said. By now he was done with washing her back. He got back up to his feet and handed the sponge back to her.

"Thanks," she said, and then stood up too. "I think I'll take a break myself. I'll have another bath when we're through talking."

She was small, her body compact and nicely built. Roman, who had now gotten over his disappointment that she wasn't his ex-girlfriend Amy, helped her out of the bathtub and then watched her towel herself dry.

"How does a human woman become a queen in hell?" he inquired as she dried her hair. At the moment, that seemed even more puzzling than the question of why she had summoned him here.

She laughed. "Same as everywhere else. Law of the jungle. Survival of the fittest. I killed the woman who was Diva here before me and usurped her position."

This was Roman's first inkling that 'Diva' was her title rather than her name. He realized that when referring to her, Breakwind had occasionally used the word 'Diva' as a title too.

"That's all?"

Diva had now finished drying her hair. Before she replied him, she replaced the wet towel on the rack. "It was more than enough. Once the Diva was dead, I took off the gold mask," she stroked her gold-plated nose demonstratively. "The mask serves us as a crown here. I removed it from her head and placed it on my own face. I've been Diva ever since."

"But you're a human woman. Don't the demons object?"

MOTEL GOTHIC

She shook her head. "Not at all. This is one of Hell's ambassadorial territories, where humans and demons mingle freely. Because of its erotic nature and its close contacts with the human realms, the ruler here is always a human; and most times is a woman. The demons don't care who it is. They respect whoever wears the mask; that's the law here."

Then she pointed to his erect penis and laughed. "I'm either gonna have to help you out with that, or have one of my girls do so. Or else you'll have blue balls in the morning."

Roman shrugged. "Don't I know it. I've already had sex once tonight and yet I feel as randy as ever."

Suddenly Diva looked sad. Although the gold mask obscured most of her face, and as such reduced her capacity to express emotion via her facial features, Roman noticed that she'd gained a sudden mournful curve to her lips. "Oh yes, you had sex with Christine Valona."

"How could you possibly know that?" he asked.

"Easy enough. Christine Valona is a conduit to the darkness. It was largely because you fucked her that I can summon you here now."

Roman felt bothered by her gloom. "Why do you look sad all of a sudden? Is there something you're not telling me?"

She quickly regained her composure and giggled. "Oh, I'll tell you later. But don't worry, it's not what you think. She doesn't have venereal disease or anything like that."

Roman heaved a sigh of relief. That had been his instant concern; that despite using protection with Christine, she may still have given him an STD.

"And you know what else? Nor do I have an STD either," Diva told Roman next, locking her fingers in his. "Come and have sex with me."

They crossed to the bed. As they did so Roman looked out of the apartment's windows. The openings provided a panoramic view of this region of hell, an arousing vagina-pink and flame-orange landscape that stretched as far as he could see. The sounds of the lusty activity outside flooded the apartment like sensual music.

"This realm is the reason you've been feeling so horny," Diva explained as they sank onto the bed together. "Happens all the time. Once I've a desire for a connection, it transmits across the realms to the object of my desire and makes them desire me in return."

Roman nodded and let her pull his shorts off. And then she took his throbbing erect phallus into her mouth and for a while he no longer cared about the reasons for anything.

The sex was surprisingly sweet, not anything like the unrestrained couplings he'd witnessed on his walk here from the motel. When he looked into Diva's blue eyes while thrusting into her, he imagined something like sadness in them. She seemed to regret something; either something she already had done or something she was destined to do. This perceived sense of loss translated itself to him and heightened the sexual experience.

Afterwards they lay sated on the bed, both sweaty from the heat, with Roman tracing the contours of Diva's golden mask with the fingers of his right hand as she lay beside him. The golden layer was a quarter of an inch thick; its edges lay flush against her skin. No space seemed to exist between metal and skin.

"Is it glued to your face?" he asked. "It looks that way to me."

She shook her head. "No, it's not glued on; the metal has replaced my skin."

He looked at her in surprise. "How is that possible?"

She kissed his cheek. "In the same way that your being here right now is possible: magic, the paranormal or supernatural; call it what you like."

"But how do you know that it's *replaced* your skin?"

She leaned up on her elbow, and regarded him. "Okay, so long as you don't mind the gruesome details." She waited till he'd nodded that she go on, then said, "Remember I told how I killed the previous Diva here and took the mask off of her? What actually happened was that once she was dead, the mask fell off her face by itself. And . . . well, she had no facial skin beneath it, nothing but raw muscle . . . and there was no skin on the mask's underside either. Crazy, huh?"

"Yeah."

"How I think it works? I think the mask eats up—absorbs if you like—the wearer's skin lying beneath the parts it covers. Considering that it won't come off again except the Diva dies, I guess it's an effective process."

Roman touched the cold metal again. "But . . . doesn't it hurt?"

She shook her head. "Not in the slightest, and the best part is, the mask conceals most of the signs of aging. I no longer have to check myself for wrinkles in the mirror."

They both laughed at that, then she added. "One side-effect of wearing the mask, however, is that it makes you ceaselessly horny. But, seeing as I'm overseeing a realm of hedonists, I guess that's a positive, what with my endless couplings with human and demon lovers. And when I'm not in the mood for company"—she gestured over at the opposite wall, at a well-furnished rack of sex toys—"I enjoy being my own best friend."

He nodded. Maybe her mask was affecting him too, or maybe it was simply a property of being here, but he was becoming erect again. While he wasn't adverse to making love with her again—she was a very satisfying woman—he wanted answers to his questions.

"So . . . why did you bring me here?" he asked, just as Diva noticed he was hard again and encircled his turgid penis with her fingers.

She kissed him on the lips. "Let's do it first and then I'll tell you."

"Tell me first, or I won't be able to concentrate."

"Fair enough." She let go of his penis and then patted it, then she snuggled up closer to him and explained, "There's nothing much to it really. As you've no doubt observed, this hell motel exactly overlays its earthly counterpart."

"Yeah. Nice name: Orgasm Motel."

"Yeah, it's cool. But don't distract me. What this overlay means is that most times I can sense who's in Earth's Sunflower Motel—Christine Valona's dying there had something to do with linking both realms this closely. Anyway, tonight I sensed you. And I really liked you and wanted to meet you."

"That's all?" Roman pulled himself up to a sitting position against the headboard and pillows, so she was lying with her head on this thigh. "That guy Breakwind made it sound like it was of utmost importance."

Diva laughed. "Well, I didn't feel like playing with myself tonight and my orgasm is of uttermost importance to me."

Roman smiled. He felt immensely relieved. Even though no harm had so far been done to him in hell, he'd been worried that the reverse might soon be the case. In the back of his mind had lurked the possibility that despite all appearances to the contrary, he had actually been lured down here to be tormented.

"Well, if that's all, I guess we should make the most of the time available." He pointed down at his penis. "You can resume playing with it now."

She giggled. "Uh uh, lover boy, this time you eat me first." Then she got up off the bed and walked over to the rack containing her sex toys. "But first I need to do something to you."

"What's that?" Roman asked, when Diva returned to the bed carrying a small bottle and an artist's paintbrush.

"I need to write a spell of protection on you," she said. When he raised eyebrows to that statement, she explained further: "You can't leave here by the same route you arrived." Leaving the bottle and brush on the bed, she strode across to the nearest of her apartment's windows and pointed out of it, down at the motel's middle block.

"Different laws govern arrivals and departures here," she continued while the rapturous noises of human-demon coupling poured through the window like audible confetti. "When you leave me in a little while, Breakwind will show you the way out. It's a short walk, and will lead you directly back to your motel room on Earth." She frowned. "But for that short period you'll still be in hell and you'll be walking alone. The spell or sign that I'll write on you will prevent any demons you happen to meet on the way from mistaking you as an escapee, and carrying you off to torment. I'd hate for that to happen to you."

"Wow, thanks," Roman said nervously. "But . . . in that case, wouldn't it be better to wait until after we get all sweaty again? I mean, in case the spell rubs off?"

Shaking her head while walking back to the bed, she said, "No problem. It'll be absorbed into your skin immediately I write it. It won't reappear until you're safely home again, and then you can wash it off with soap and water."

"I get that, but why not wait anyway?"

She giggled. "Because, honey, once we get through having sex again, I intend to have another milk bath and then fall fast asleep. I'm already a little dozy now, but not enough to confuse me. I don't trust myself to make the right inscriptions later, and one wrongly written word could endanger your life."

Roman nodded and she uncapped the bottle (which contained black ink) and got to work. It didn't take long to do. She painted some words on his chest, drew a circle with six upside-down crosses inside it below those, and then wrote more words beneath that on his belly.

Once done, she whispered something and the whole inscription vanished. Roman felt its disappearance into himself as if he'd just taken a long and deep breath. Then he felt normal again.

"And now let's get back to fucking," Diva said, capping the paint bottle again.

This time they went at it with more energy than previously. Roman ate her until she came and then he thrust into her hard till she screamed so much that he realized she was putting on a performance for her citizens/subjects outside. During her orgasm, her apartment's lighting reflected off her golden mask with blinding intensity.

"Hey, what's your name?" he asked afterward, as they rested in a peaceful afterglow moment.

"You already know it," she replied sleepily. "I'm Diva."

"No, that's just your title. I mean your real name."

She sighed. "My real name doesn't matter. What does is that I am Diva now, queen and ruler of all this great realm of hell. We Divas are as interchangeable as tires. Last year another woman was Diva here, next year someone else may be, but we are all Diva."

"I don't understand that last bit."

"There's huge competition for the gold mask and the rules are simple: kill whoever currently rules and take their place. I rule now, but only for as long as I can fend off my competitors. The day I become lax, I'll be killed and another will put on my mask and rule here."

"I get it," he said. He felt a deep liking for her, this sex queen of the not-so-damned. "It's a sad fate."

"I chose it," she said, with a yawn. "And no, it's not sad. I don't regret my choice. If I die today, it'll have been worth it. The power . . . the sex . . ."

He nodded. "Yeah, if you say so."

She winked at him. "Time for you to go, stud. As much as I've enjoyed meeting and plowing you, I've a schedule to keep to."

He laughed. "A schedule?"

She laughed too. "Yeah, a schedule. Sex, sex, and more sex. Being Diva here means I can't refuse anyone's erotic requests; I have to offer satisfaction to every citizen in the Sex Realm." She yawned again. "Needless to say, it's exhausting." She glanced across at the wall, at a clock with weird markings, runes instead of numbers. "It's about three a.m. now, your time." She leaned up on her elbow and then rolled over him to the edge of the bed. Once out of bed, she reached out a hand to him and helped him up also. He watched his sperm drool down her right thigh.

He picked up his shorts and was about pulling them on when she stopped him.

"Wait, let's get you cleaned up first," she instructed.

They walked together to the milk-filled bathtub. Roman tested the temperature of the milk with a finger. It was still warm.

"Incredible, huh?" Diva asked on seeing the surprise on his face. "One of the perks of this place."

Roman nodded.

"Step up to the edge of the tub," Diva said. Roman did so and she scooped up handfuls of milk and washed his penis and scrotum with the warm liquid.

Afterwards, while he pulled on his shorts, she climbed into the bathtub and lowered herself down into the milk.

"So how do I leave?" Roman asked. "He'd begun feeling sleepy too, and needed to get into bed as soon as possible.

"In a minute," she replied, scooping milk over her breasts with both hands, and then feeling about for her sponge. "Before you go, Roman, I want to tell you a secret about your future," she nodded at his inquiring gaze. "Yes, you heard me right. I want to tell you your future."

He'd had no idea she was psychic too. And with the way she was yawning now, he suspected she would shortly fall asleep inside her bathtub. "Okay, I'm listening," he said.

"There isn't much to tell," she said. "But I do know this—in a short while, you're going to be extremely happy, happier than you've been for ages. But unfortunately, your happiness will be brief, very brief indeed."

As Diva said this, Roman once again had the feeling that she was sad about something. Beneath her golden nose, her lips tried to smile but failed miserably.

Is she scared she's going to die soon? But no, she's telling my fortune, not hers.

He looked at her, his eyes requesting for more information, but she simply shook her head back at him. "That's all I can see, man: that you'll be ecstatically, blissfully happy, but your happiness will be very short-lived."

He frowned and shrugged and thought again about Amy Watkins. "Story of my life, baby," he told Diva. "Story of my fucking life. For me, holding on to happiness is like grasping the air. Maybe I'm cursed."

Barely awake now, she just managed to comment: "Oh, don't take it so badly. I can assure you that a few moments of ecstasy well outweighs a lifetime of sorrow. Take me, for instance. If another witch successfully launches a coup against me tonight, I may be dead before morning. But in the meantime, my life is simply wonderful; an endless orgy." She yawned again. "Damn, Roman, you were good; I haven't felt this sleepy in ages."

Then she pointed to the hallway that led downstairs. "Go back the way you came. Find Breakwind. He'll show you the way home. And remember to wash off the protection spell once you're back home. Soap and water will do it."

With those words Diva fell asleep in the stone bathtub. Roman bent and kissed the forehead of her golden mask and then left her apartment.

I'll be blissfully happy for a while, but then sadness? Yeah, that sounds just like me.

As to her instruction to wash off the protection spell, recalling how extensively she'd painted the now-disappeared inscription on his chest and belly, he didn't see how he could possibly forget to clean it off.

Roman found Breakwind down in the reception lobby, having sex with Mamasi, the ten-breasted demoness who'd filled Diva's bathtub with milk. The couple who'd previously been having sex there—the hanging woman and her demon partner—had since left the lobby.

Breakwind and Mamasi were going at it doggy-style and the ground all around them was covered with milk, with more liquid squirting from Mamasi's breasts each time Breakwind thrust his horny penis into her; the fat demoness seemed unable to control her milk flow during intercourse.

Roman waved to Breakwind, who indicated that he wait.

To pass the time till the copulating couple were done, Roman walked over to speak to the receptionist. Her previous sexual companion had also left; her X-frame was vacant.

The demoness swung the tip of her tale suggestively at Roman. "You ready to get that raincheck whipping now?"

He shook his head and then studied her for a while. Other than for her black fangs and snakelike eyes, she was quite pretty; and her red skin glowed like a freshly polished pair of shoes. But then he focused on the split end of her tail, which she frisked left and right like a feather duster; each of its tendrils was about a foot long and as scaly as a lizard's tail.

No way is that thing being applied to my body by this chick. She looks very muscular, like she's been whipping folks' butts since she popped out of the womb, or wherever demonesses come from.

She was still eyeing him seductively. He shook his head at her. "Sorry, baby, I'll have to raincheck the raincheck. I think I see my old college lecturer Professor Montez out there; wonder what the old lecher's doing here."

"Same thing as everyone else is, honey," the demoness replied with a disappointed pout. "All there is to do here in Sex Realm is fuck."

"And whip, of course," Roman added.

She brightened up a little. "Hey, ask your professor if he'd like to be whipped *two*, as in, me doing both of you at once," she said, slapping the tendrilled end of her tail on her desk for emphasis; her cute little batwings flapped as if independently excited.

Roman had lied just now; Professor Montez wasn't out there. But there was a whole lot of sexual carrying-on visible through the open door; and even more abundant than sights to titillate even the most jaded voyeur were the sounds, that perpetual soundtrack of lust the like of which porn could never imagine or hope to reproduce. Thankfully, Roman wasn't erect again—three orgasms in one night seemed to have calmed his loins . . . for now. He understood that it was merely a matter of time before he grew erect again. There was eroticism in the air here; and the view and noises were such as would make a monk or nun regret taking their holy vows.

Still clearly disappointed at not having her way with his body, the red receptionist tweaked her nipples, which were large as thumb-tips and as black as coal, protruding from her red breasts like the tops of extinct volcanoes. "For me, whipping someone is even better than fucking them," she declared seriously.

"I wish I felt the same way," Roman said.

"You can if you want to," she countered. "You ever been whipped before?"

He shook his head. "No, but it looks painful."

She nodded. "It *is* painful. That's the whole point of it; but your brain interprets the pain as pleasure. I know that sounds silly, but in practice, it's very nice. I just tie you up on this frame here and then I beat you and you start feeling good."

Roman's next comment was drowned out by a loud noise from behind him, which turned out to be the multiple-breasted demoness's orgasm. He turned around to watch. Mamasi was riding Breakwind now and as she climaxed, milk squirted from her breasts at high pressure, streamed straight over Breakwind's chest and head, and whitewashed the nearby wall. Roman was very impressed by the force of the milk jets.

"Mamasi is such a show-off," the flagellating receptionist remarked sourly, sucking on an index claw. "But Diva loves taking milk baths, so she's her favorite. You know, I really wish Diva liked being whipped too. But no, she's like you—says she's not into that masochism shit."

"I wonder why that is?" Roman said. Behind them Mamasi's orgasm was slowly subsiding into a series of soft moans.

His red companion's eyes narrowed, and the ends of her lips curled downward. "Hey, man, are you making fun of me?"

Roman quickly shook his head. "Hey, I've an idea: how 'bout if I whip *you* instead? Your tail looks long enough for me to whip you with it. Then, when I'm convinced *you're* enjoying it, we can trade places. How 'bout that?"

Her brow furrowed as she considered his proposition.

"Don't bother, dude," Breakwind said, joining them at the reception desk. He clapped a hand on Roman's shoulder. "Demon skin is so thick and horny that whipping her won't make the slightest impact. It'll be like tickling her."

"Oh, you damn spoilsport," the receptionist said and punched Breakwind playfully in the chest. "I just wanted to broaden his vanilla horizons."

"Yeah, yeah, I know," Breakwind said. The demon was dripping wet with milk, and in addition to this, Roman also noticed that Breakwind was wheezing like he was out of breath, something he'd never have expected from a demon. He didn't think they could get exhausted; at least not after sex.

"Hey, Diva said you'll show me the way out of here. I need to get back to Earth," Roman said. "You know, before someone misses me?"

"Oh, you should have said so earlier," the receptionist said. She pointed past him. "You just head out the back door, and you're back in the Earth version of this motel."

"Out the back door? Won't that simply return me outside?"

Breakwind shook his head. "No, it's a special door. Come on, I'll lead you to the passageway."

"Be seeing you, Roman," the receptionist told him when he waved goodbye to her. "Remember, that's now two rainchecked whippings I owe you."

He nodded. "Yeah sure, next time I'm in hell, my body is yours to do whatever you like with."

His words pleased her; she was grinning when he headed away after Breakwind, who was already halfway across the lobby.

"Watch out for the milk!" the receptionist laughed.

This was no idle joke; the pool of breast milk extended halfway across the lobby.

Roman looked at Mamasi. With a broad smile on her face, the demoness lay asleep at the far end of the milk lake.

Roman gaped at something: the demoness had an eye in her anus; the eye was blinking between the crack of her buttocks.

His surprise was cut short by Breakwind, who elbowed him in the ribs, nodded towards Mamasi and whispered: "I noticed the questioning look on your face earlier. Hey, let me tell you something, dude: this fat girl here might not look like it, but she's the best fuck I've ever had. Trust me, where sex is concerned, looks are far from everything."

"Yeah, sure," Roman agreed. "Why're you whispering?"

Breakwind jerked a thumb over his shoulder, at the receptionist. "It's never wise to praise one woman's bedroom prowess in the presence of another; particularly not one you've also slept with."

They walked through the milk (there was no way to avoid it splashing their feet) and stepped into the rear hallway again.

This time Breakwind led Roman past the stairwell that led to Diva's quarters. Roman thought he heard Diva snoring on the upper floor.

One difference here was the lack of sexual sound. The farther they proceeded down the rear hallway, the quieter their environment became, until they were standing in silence before a grey door.

"Here's your way home," Breakwind told Roman, then he pulled it open, revealing a corridor. "Follow it to the end and you'll be back in your room again."

The corridor beyond the door was hazy; Roman couldn't make out its end. For a few seconds he felt indecisive about stepping into it, but then he remembered the protection spell Diva had written on his chest. He imagined he could feel it inside him now, an invisible shield beneath his skin. The imagery strengthened him; he knew that even if he lost his way, he could easily return to this door again.

However, Roman had a question before he entered the corridor:

"Assuming I'd like to return here sometime," he asked Breakwind. "How do I go about doing so?"

Breakwind scratched a long canine tooth. "About the only *guaranteed* way you can get here—without the Diva summoning you the way she did tonight—is if you begin practicing black magic. You now know that this motel overlays the one on Earth. It's a permanent overlay too. But opening the door to this side isn't easy; there's all sorts of rituals, blood sacrifices . . ."

Roman gaped at him. "So all those people I saw out there, they're . . . they're all into witchcraft?"

Breakwind laughed. "Yeah, dude. Even with the temptation of endless sex, who else but a witch wants to come to hell; even for a visit?"

Roman stepped into the corridor and the demon shut the door behind him.

CHAPTER 14

Dooks

After a further short period of ruminating on his options in the armchair, Harry Dooks made up his mind on what he would do.

He opened his eyes and frowned at Manface. "I'll take the money, mutt. I don't believe I'll die if I do."

The dog-demon scowled back at him. "You will."

"I'll take my chances that you're lying about that. You're just bullshitting me."

Manface didn't look angry, just disappointed. "Okay then, Harry, it's your funeral. Tell me what you wish for."

"I wish for a billion dollars," Dooks said. Saying it after all this while felt very anticlimactic; all of the killing, anticipation and deliberation had sucked the thrill from the juicy moment.

And besides, nothing happened. Dooks didn't know what he'd expected to happen anyway. A lightning flash? The sudden appearance of hundreds of stacks of hundred dollar bills? Though of course, a billion dollars couldn't possibly fit in this room.

It was just so anticlimactic.

Manface seemed to concentrate for a few seconds, its borrowed eyes staring hard into space, and then it said. "Done. Congratulations, Harry, you're a rich man now, if a dead one."

Dooks extend his hands towards the demon, palms up, fingers spread in a confused gesture. "So, where's the money, mutt? I don't see anything."

Manface laughed. "Don't worry about that. The cash will come; six months from now, you'll have a billion in the bank. You played the Devil's Coin Game and won, so that's guaranteed. The problem is, you *don't have* six months from now. Harry, you don't seem to get it— I'm not lying to you. You don't have even six hours from now left to live."

Dooks felt some fear on hearing this, but he'd already decided not to listen to the demon, so he shrugged off his resurgent worries. "You could be lying to me. Give me some proof that I'll be as rich as you claim."

Manface nodded. "I was just about to, Harry. Do you remember what I told you about Christine Valona; how the million dollars she stole was never found?"

Dooks nodded slowly. "Yeah. What's that got to do with me?"

Manface smiled. "The money's here, Harry. Here in this motel."

Dooks gaped at Manface. "Here?" He glanced around the room. "In this room?"

"No, not here in this room. The money is hidden in the janitor's storage room, down the block. Where your dead friend over there kept his cleaning supplies. There's an improvised panel on the rear wall there, for a AC unit that was removed when the place was converted to a storage room. Christine hid the money in the space behind the panel."

Dooks recalled that Hicks was—had been—the Sunflower Motel's janitor. "Are you sure?"

"*Dead* serious. Take the key from your friend's pocket and head over there. You'll need a screwdriver too, to get the panel open. Don't look so surprised: Hicks fucked Christine lots of times; she was his favorite prostitute. The night Christine arrived here from Springfield with the stolen money, Hicks was drunk. He had no idea what she'd done. Christine took his keys, stashed the cash in the wall—she had more than enough time to do so—and then she tried to get away and leave town. She was caught near the reception building; and that's where they killed her; though they didn't intend to.

"The guys Huggers had sent after Christine weren't expecting her to put up the fight she did. But Christine was a tough girl. She'd been expecting trouble and had a gun. She shot one goon dead and the other one stabbed her to death while she was trying to shoot him too. That done, he had no chance to search for the money; he loaded his dead friend into their car and drove off before the cops arrived." Manface laughed. "Huggers never realized Christine left the cash here; if he had he'd have turned the motel upside-down to find it. Huggers still thinks Christine already offloaded the cash onto a friend of hers before arriving here and his guys caught her while she was trying to book a room for the night."

Dooks was already on his feet and heading for Hicks, though he didn't relish rifling through the dead man's pockets, especially not since a good chunk of Hicks's innards lay across them on the armchair.

He liked looking at Hicks's head even less. The sight was beyond creepy to behold. *Exactly how does a man's entire face get transplanted somewhere else? It's a good thing Manface is taking Hicks and Robby to hell with him when he leaves, or else it's gonna be the fucking X-Files here when their corpses are discovered.*

"Not *those* pockets, Harry," Manface said, just as Dooks began pushing aside Hicks's spilled intestines. It waited until Dooks had abandoned his search and turned back to it, before adding, while gesturing left with its eyes, "In the lower right pocket of his coveralls."

The blue coveralls hung on a peg by the closet. Dooks had to step over Robby to reach it.

That was unpleasant as the blood from Robby's head and the blood from his chest and belly now darkened the rug for quite an expanse, making it sticky on the feet. But Dooks managed it, avoiding the reach of the blood by balancing on his toes. He got the key ring out of Hicks's pocket and backed away across the floor.

Then he walked past Manface to the front door.

"Where exactly are you going?" the demon asked nicely.

"I'm off to get the briefcase."

"Looking like that? Harry, you look like a serial killer who's just murdered a family of four."

Dooks, enthused by thoughts of soon holding a million dollars in his hands, paused with his fingers on the door handle. He realized the demon was right. He was quite the mess now; covered in blood from head to feet. Anyone seeing him would immediately call the police.

I need new clothes. I can wipe my shoes clean, but for pants and a shirt I'll need to raid Hicks's closet. All his clothes are certain to be XXXL, but maybe, just maybe I'll find something left over from before he grew a beer gut.

Ignoring both the frozen dog-creature on the sofa and Hicks on the armchair opposite it, Dooks stepped over Robby again.

He reached Hicks's closet and then realized he first needed to wash the blood off his hands before opening it; or else he would stain the clothes in the closet. So he headed back towards the bathroom.

One look in the bathroom mirror convinced him of the wisdom of not stepping outside until he'd cleaned himself up. A bright splash of blood covered the left side of his face, extending down his chin and covering his shirt. The fringe of dirty-blonde hair near his left ear was bloodstained too. Now that he applied his mind to it, he thought the blood had gotten on his head while he'd been butchering Robby.

Yeah, that must be when it happened. It if had happened while I was cutting up Hicks, Robby would have joked about it.

He washed his hands quickly, then soaked a towel in water and soaped the mess off of his face and neck. This led to him stripping off his shirt so he could wash his hair and chest and belly clean.

Once Dooks no longer looked like a maniac, he urinated in the toilet and then reentered the main room.

"You don't need to be in such a hurry," Manface told him while he searched the closet for something that would fit him.

"What you talking 'bout, mutt?" he called back. "The sooner I'm done here, the better."

"I'm talking about keeping you alive," was the reply. "I've a plan to do so."

Dooks paused his search. "Keep talking, mutt."

"Come back over here where I can see you. I can't move, remember?"

Dooks unhooked a medium-sized tee shirt from a hanger and laid it out on the bed. Then he walked back over to the living room area and sat down facing the demon. "Go on, mutt."

"Harry, I can sense something about to happen here in the motel. If it happens like I think it will, then, in return for a favor from you, I will grant you one more wish, which of course will keep you alive to enjoy your money."

"What do you expect to happen? Are you sure this is going to work?"

"It's something magical. Just be patient. In half an hour we'll know for sure."

Dooks wanted to call Manface's bluff, but he didn't dare, because the demon didn't appear to be bluffing him. Though it addressed him with cold calm, he clearly sensed excitement in its voice.

What on Earth does it expect to happen?

Dooks had no answer. But the simple fact that by waiting like the demon was asking him to, he might ensure his own survival beyond the morning, convinced him to go along with Manface's suggestion.

"I'll wait like you say," he told Manface.

"Good. I don't think you'll regret it. If you still don't feel like staying alive afterwards, you can wish for another billion dollars, instead of a long life."

"Shut up, mutt." After a look at the time, Dooks got up and walked back over to Hicks's closet to search for a pair of pants that might fit him.

He still had plenty of time. There were still three hours till daybreak.

CHAPTER 15

Roman

Roman was experiencing spatial displacement. Although he had so far not encountered any lurking demons in the corridor meant to return him to his motel room, the passageway itself seemed inordinately long. Its walls were of unbroken gray stone, and as Roman walked between them, he recalled how back at the entrance to this place, the corridor's end had been shrouded in mist like something unformed. This made him wonder if indeed the corridor was being formed as he walked along it, new lengths being added just out of range of his vision.

Where the hell is it taking me? Should I just turn around now and go back to Diva and Breakwind in hell?

However, although the prospect of endless and unrestrained sex greatly appealed to him, so did the prospect of getting back to the world he understood. He didn't doubt that if he did turn around and return to Diva's Sex Realm, she would welcome him with parted thighs; and then, once she had had her fill of him again, would happily pass him on to that pretty receptionist demoness with the whipping fetish.

The fear of being whipped by that split tail was sufficient motivation for Roman to proceed with his journey.

Maybe, like Breakwind mentioned, I'll just take some courses in black magic and find out how to return to the Sex Realm whenever I feel like it.

And so Roman Fowler continued on his trip back home.

Now, however, he thought he heard voices up ahead. Hearing these sounds gave him additional motivation to keep walking forward, even though both the mist up ahead and the tunnel that it might be creating still seemed endless.

CHAPTER 16

Tenebra

Once she had gotten all the candles lit, Tenebra turned off the lights in her motel room and then took a few moments to consider her handiwork.

There, it's done, she thought with satisfaction, a cruel smile spreading over her face.

The ritual required implanting six candles in human flesh and then lighting them.

She grinned down at the surviving fool who had come here to assassinate her. Mandy lay on her back squirming in pain as the burning candles dropped their hot wax on her tormented flesh. As far as Tenebra could see, Mandy was already out of her mind; she'd completely lost all sense of who she was and why she was here. Now her gaze was comprised entirely of pain and suffering; her eyes held no more comprehension than those of a deer dying after being hit by a truck.

It must have been when I took that shit in her vagina, Tenebra thought, her eyes glittering with pure unrestrained evil as she studied a telltale smear of excrement on Mandy's labia. *That would break anyone's mind.* Then she laughed. *So remind me to do it more often to bitches I hate.*

She didn't care at all about the cringing young woman at her feet. *It's her fault that she's here and she deserves everything she's getting.*

Tenebra's sole irritation at the moment was that she hadn't stuck all six candles in Mandy's body. But this was purely an aesthetic displeasure and not a ritual one. Mandy had four burning candles in her: one in each breast, one in her navel, and the one plugging her vagina. She had looked so nice like this that Tenebra hadn't wanted to ruin this macabre work of art she'd created by sticking two additional candles elsewhere in her body.

I should have stuck one up her ass also, and a very large one at that. But the angle would have been wrong and I'd have wound up setting the rug on fire.

The fifth burning candle was the huge one stuck in Dewdrop's back; the sixth was being held by headless Kelli.

(Rather than make a hole in Kelli's body, Tenebra had peeled all of the skin off of Kelli's palms and made her hold the candle with the fingers of both hands interlocked. While not an actual implantation in flesh, Tenebra knew what the ritual actually required was for the base of each candle to be wrapped in raw human flesh, so this worked too.)

The other important detail for the ritual was the large black pentagram Tenebra had drawn on the wall opposite the front door. Coincidentally, the pentagram was positioned directly over Kelli's decapitated head, but the head's location had nothing to do with the ritual. Tenebra simply didn't know where else to put the head. It wasn't doing any harm where it was, so she'd left it there. It looked rather cute there.

So much blood everywhere around me now.

Tenebra was not entirely without feelings, however. As she looked around the room, ensuring she was ready to complete the ritual that would open for her the portal to the Sex Realm, she recalled that the pair of would-be assassins had been lovers.

Oh, it had been so long since Tenebra had really been in love.

"Not since Roman," she said aloud, addressing herself to the squirming pain-crazed young woman on the floor. "Now that was a love worth dying for. I don't doubt that Roman would have gladly taken a bullet for me, or even"—here she bent over and tapped all three candles in Mandy's torso, with the effect of starting fresh streams of tears from her captive's eyes—"if Roman had been here tonight, he'd have gladly let you two bitches behead him if he'd thought it would ensure my survival. That was how much he loved me."

She straightened up again and sadness covered her face. "But what happened? What went wrong in our fairytale romance? Nothing really, and yet *everything* was wrong—like I already told you. In one sense leaving Roman was the biggest mistake I ever made." Tenebra sighed and continued addressing her captive. "And yet, it really wasn't. You can't live forever as just half of what you truly are. I was living a total lie, and eventually it would have come out that there was a whole lot more to me than my darling thought there was. And what then? When Roman knew who I really was, I'd lose the same love that I'd been lying to protect." She flicked the candle in Mandy's left breast again, this time with her toes. "So I left Roman. I've no doubt that I broke his heart, but . . . it simply couldn't be helped. Would I do the same again? I don't know. I'd like to think I wouldn't, but . . ."

Tenebra grinned. "But of course, there's compensations in everything. Like now. Once I cast this spell, I'm on my way to the Sex Realm to kill the currently reigning Diva and take over her throne. The portal leads directly to her back door. And of course, the bitch has no idea I'm gunning for her. I'll be a queen before daybreak."

Tenebra knew Mandy couldn't respond even if she took her gag off; she was too far gone, pain had fully eclipsed her mind. But that was the entire point of telling Mandy: she was the perfect listener; one who could never reveal secrets. Tenebra felt she had to get the truth about Roman Fowler off her chest. She had borne this emotional burden, kept her secret to herself, for too long. And now, right when she was about leaving the human world for good, seemed the best time to let someone share her feelings.

"The best part of this is, once I'm Diva, I can actually have Roman brought to me in the Sex Realm. And then we'll live happily ever after." She laughed. "Unlike you, Mandy, who are about to die messily now."

Remembering how much Roman had loved her always put Tenebra (aka Amy Watkins) in a funk. It angered her that since leaving him she'd never been able to reproduce that kind of transcending emotional connection with anyone else—either male or female. She didn't doubt that given time, she might have met someone just as right for her, but in the interim all those she'd dated were simply after her body or her beauty, or, since she'd become very adept at witchcraft, the magical advantages that being her lover would afford them. These continual romantic failures had hardened Tenebra, had drained her of empathy. After all, if no really cared about her, why should she in turn care about others?

Tenebra had initially felt that Petra Velli might be the right woman for her; but now she admitted to herself that she'd been very naïve. Though she practiced serial adultery as a hobby, Petra was slavishly devoted to her husband and so the relationship with her girlfriend had fizzled out. A lesbian relationship had no future when one of the partners constantly looked forward to hurrying home so her mobster husband could fuck her in the ass.

And now the bitch sent assassins to kill me. How fucking wrong can you be about someone?

Tenebra kicked Mandy out of frustration. *I know exactly how to repay Petra. Once I'm Diva in the Sex Realm, I'll have Petra brought there and . . . Okay, that's enough daydreaming!*

Yes, it was time to complete the ritual. After a final glance at the pentagram on the wall, and stroking her amulet for comfort, she picked up her black knife from the table and approached Mandy.

Trapped in her own universe of suffering, Mandy watched Tenebra approach with blank eyes. She didn't flinch even when Tenebra paused beside her and raised the long black knife above her head.

But Tenebra wasn't about using the knife on Mandy. Instead, swaying in the combination of light and shadows created by the candles stuck in Mandy's body, she began intoning a spell:

"Latrop eht emoceb d'na pu pir

Latrop eht emoceb d'na pu raet

L'leh ot!"

She repeated this thrice and then stepped back.

Oh yes, it's happening!

In the flickering candlelight Mandy's pink skin had begun flowing like water over her body. But this was merely the preamble. Next, while Mandy gaped in horrified incomprehension, her skin began tearing off of her body. There was nothing neat or beautiful about this; Mandy's skin ripped off in large and little pieces which then streaked through the air, towards the pentagram Tenebra had drawn on the wall. Next, in a spray of blood, Mandy's muscles followed suit, messily tearing off of her bones in a fountain of meat and flying through the air after her recently departed skin. Her facial skin was already stuck on the wall, and now her eyes popped from her sockets and travelled after it, along with all the flesh on her face; after which her tongue tore free from between her jaws and went airborne also.

In thirty seconds it was over. The erstwhile young murderess lay dead on the floor, a stripped skeleton in a pool of blood, with just her internal organs left inside her ribcage and draped over her spinal column; the four candles still in place and burning bright.

Meanwhile, over on the wall, there now existed a giant bleeding pentagram made of her skin and flesh.

After smirking at the new corpse, Tenebra turned to the pentagram on the wall and intoned:

"M'laer xes eh tot rood eht pu nepo!"

As though it was being unscrewed, the meat pentagram began spinning anticlockwise. Six revolutions later it vanished, leaving an arched portal in the wall. The portal was rimmed with Mandy's flesh and led into a stone-walled tunnel which swirled with smoke as if fire burnt somewhere inside it.

Tenebra smiled coldly to herself. *Yes, I did it!*

All that remained now was to pack up her bags and head into hell. No point in getting dressed first. Just like she'd explained to the sacrificed girl, no one bothered with clothes in hell's Sex Realm.

Tenebra was just about to start packing, when she noticed someone in the tunnel, approaching her motel room.

What the hell? Immediately on her guard in case it was some kind of guardian demon (though her spellbook hadn't warned about any of those), she stood facing the opening with her knife held at the ready to strike; though of course demons couldn't step out into the human realm except one invited them.

But it wasn't any demon approaching. Tenebra couldn't believe her eyes when she saw just who was about stepping out of hell into her motel room.

Roman? Roman Fowler? What's HE doing here?

CHAPTER 17

Roman

Right at the point when Roman began thinking it was time to retrace his steps to the Orgasm Motel, the doorway appeared in front of him.

An arched portal materialized where seconds before there had been nothing but swirling smoky mist. Even though this portal was bordered by bleeding human flesh, Roman, who was tired of walking about in a seeming limbo, hurried forward to enter the room beyond it.

However, even before stepping over the doorway's fleshy threshold, he could see that something was wrong. First off, he'd left no corpses behind in his own motel room. And second, there also hadn't been a naked woman in his motel room when he'd left there.

But his worries about the bloodshed everywhere paled into total insignificance when he recognized the woman who was standing in the room and gaping back at him in equal confusion.

"Amy?" he gasped, his heart seeming to skip several beats. "What . . . what . . . what are you doing h-h-here?"

"I'm about asking you the same question," Amy Watkins replied, with a confused joy on her face that he knew matched his own facial expression.

She was already hurrying towards him and he was doing the same; striding forward at his heart's direction, six steps brought him to her. And next she was in his arms once again after a whole year apart and he was weeping and kissing her in delight.

There was no doubting her own passion either as her lips and tongue explored his.

But even while Roman's heart brimmed over with pleasure, he sensed something was wrong here. The problem wasn't the three corpses in the room. Despite the gore everywhere and Amy looking like she'd just escaped from a serial killer, Roman knew Amy would have a logical explanation for everything. He was certain the corpses were those of Amy's abductors, the evil villains who'd torn her away from him.

Roman had never been this happy before; he doubted he'd ever feel this happy again. Being reunited the woman he loved, after all this time! Yes, he was certain he would never feel this happy again.

"Oh my God, Roman," Amy wept while kissing him with her arms tightly wrapped around his neck. "You've no idea how often I've longed to be in your arms again! I was just thinking about you!"

"And me too, darling," Roman gushed back at her. "I've missed you oh so much!"

But something *was* very wrong. Then Roman realized what it was: the spell of protection that Diva had painted on his body was leaving him. He at first felt like something was peeling off his bones and muscles. And then he felt it streak out of him and hit Amy in the breasts and belly. The sensation had been physical, as if he'd punched her.

That baffled Roman.

And Amy had clearly felt it too. She'd broken her intense lip-lock with him and had staggered back and was now gasping for breath. With one hand reaching out to him, she gasped, "Roman, where . . . where are you coming from? What happ . . . ? Who did . . . ?" Then she looked down at her body and howled in horror.

Roman gaped now. Diva's spell now decorated *both* of their bodies. And now, instead of its original black color, the inscription was flashing bright red.

Amy grabbed a candle from the hands of a headless woman, who then fell to the ground.

"What's going on?" Roman asked as she ran past him and by the light of the candle began ransacking her bags for something.

"Diva set you up to destroy me," was the angry reply.

"She said it was to protect me," Roman said. But he knew Amy was telling the truth. His body now felt weird, like strange forces were at play inside of it, forces that wanted to force their way out of him; the words on his chest felt like worms wriggling in his skin and muscles.

Amy turned from her bags to stare at him. The fear in her eyes horrified him. "Diva lied to you, darling. What she painted on you wasn't a protection spell but a curse. Somehow the bitch discovered I was coming to kill her tonight and she got to you first." She turned away from him and emptied the contents of her purse on her bed. "I'll explain the details later. I need to neutralize her curse or we'll both be dea—"

That was the last thing Amy Watkins ever said. Suddenly her belly and chest both split open and the entire mass of her innards squirted out of her and flew across the room to splat against the window drapes. With her emptied torso looking like a red bathtub that was draining blood, she stared empty-eyed at Roman and then collapsed down dead, with her spilling blood extinguishing the candle she'd dropped onto the rug.

Roman watched this in horror. He started to go to Amy, but then tripped over the headless female body. By the time he'd staggered up to his feet again, the pressures in his body had reached their peak and the same thing that had just happened to Amy was happening to him too.

Roman was too surprised to even scream when the entirety of his torso split apart like double doors being violently flung open, and forces he didn't understand wrenched him completely around and then tore his heart, lungs and viscera out of his body and flung them across the room onto the TV.

Roman sank to the floor, dying, but recalling Diva's prediction of his future: "You'll be ecstatically, blissfully happy, but your happiness will be very short-lived."

As he died, he felt grateful to Diva for the two minutes of bliss he'd had of being reunited with Amy Watkins.

CHAPTER 18

Dooks and Manface

"Okay, you're in luck," Manface told Dooks.

"I still don't know what the fuck you're talking about," Dooks retorted impatiently. "You said to wait thirty minutes and it's now thirty-two minutes later."

"Cool it. It takes time for things to go right. You know that. And anyway, you spent most of the time changing your clothes."

Dooks sighed. "Okay, mutt, I'm sorry." He gestured around the room. "But I just don't like sitting here with these corpses. They're making me very uncomfortable."

Manface laughed. "In that case you're going to *love* what I've got in store for you now."

"Huh?"

"Listen," the demon told Dooks, "At the moment there are five corpses in Room 13 of this very motel. I want you to go over there and fetch all of their hearts for me. You do that and I'll grant you one more wish."

Dooks stared incredulously at the demon. "You want *what?*"

Manface smiled Robby's drunken smile at Dooks. "You heard me right. Go over to Room 13 and bring me all five human hearts in the room. Once I eat them your problems are over."

The demon spoke with intense relish, as if it could already taste the delicious human flesh on its tongue.

Dooks had no idea what to think. Outside the rain was picking up again, beating on the roof and interrupting his reasoning.

"What are you waiting for?" Manface asked.

"No, you're crazy," Dooks told the demon. "This is crazy, *you're* crazy. . . . *I'm* crazy for even waiting to listen to you." He got up from his chair.

"Where are you going?" Manface asked as he reached the door.

"I'm going to get the million dollars stashed in that air-conditioning duct and then I'm leaving here."

"Listen to me for a minute, will you?"

Despite his better judgment, Dooks did turn to look at Manface. He really did want to leave this place though. In addition to the fact that there were two faceless corpses in the room, staring at Manface itself made him queasy. There was only so much viewing of that impossible juxtaposition of human face on frozen canine sculpture that he could take before he'd run mad.

Even calling the thing 'mutt' wasn't helping his rationalization much anymore.

And what exactly happened to Brownie anyway? Is he still alive inside that statue, or did the ritual kill him? It was an additional unpleasant feeling— that they might have unwittingly sacrificed the dog.

But still, he paused with his hand on the doorknob. "Okay, I'll listen, but nothing you'll say will make any difference."

"Fair enough. Before I go on, open the door a little bit. Just take a peek."

"Why should I?"

"Just open the door, Harry."

Dooks opened the door a little bit. Then feeling chills trickling down his back, he instantly shut the door again.

"What is *she* doing out there?" he asked in a very small voice. 'She' meant Christine Valona. The 'dead' woman had been standing outside in the rain, staring at this very motel room.

"She's listening to us, Harry, to see if we reach an agreement. It's simple. You leave this room without accepting my offer to extend your life and you won't reach that storage room alive. Christine will be able to tick off another number on her soul collection quota. But she can't interfere with you until my transactions with you are finished. Do you get me?"

"I get you," Dooks nodded, feeling as numb as if he'd been shot full of morphine.

"Something else to encourage you, Harry," Manface said. "Do you know that of the five dead people in Room 13, four of them saw Christine Valona on their arrival here tonight? The sole person who didn't see her was the witch—the one you were looking at earlier through the window."

"What?" Dooks said. "She's dead too?"

"Yes, Harry, she's dead too. Room 13 was her room."

"I'll do it," Dooks said, feeling a deep pang of regret on recalling how attractive the young woman at the window had been. "I'll fetch their hearts for you." But really it seemed mission impossible, and he told the demon why: "Mutt, it's gonna take me ages to cut five hearts out of their bodies. It's not like I'm an Aztec priest."

"It won't take that long," Manface replied. "Three of the bodies are already opened up, all you have to do is locate their hearts and bag them. You'll only have to cut open the other two bodies, and those shouldn't take you long, not after all the practice you've already had tonight." Manface laughed loudly. "Then just bring them all back here to me and we're done."

"Why don't I simply carry you over there instead?" Dooks enquired. "Making the trip there and back is twice as risky, particularly considering what I'll be carrying on the return trip. And besides, if I carry you there, I can feed you the hearts as I cut them out."

Manface sighed. "That's impossible. Though you're correct that it would make things simpler."

"Why impossible?"

"Because I'm fused to this couch. You'll find it impossible to shift me."

Dooks stared at the demon. As far as he could see, both body and head couldn't weight more than forty pounds max. He debated trying to move the demon, but then decided to take Manface at his word and head over to Room 13 alone.

"One last thing before I go," he said. "How do I get the door open?"

"No problem. I'll take care of that for you; the door will be open when you get there. Just remember, don't walk on the corridor on your way back. Walk in the parking lot in case your shoes are bloody."

Dooks nodded, grabbed up his knife from the bloody tabletop, picked up a black plastic bag from near Hicks's bed, and then stepped outside before he thought twice about it.

To his relief the ghost was nowhere in sight. With the rain in his face, he ran across to the edge of the middle block, and stepped up onto its corridor. All the doors along the block were closed, and no light spilled out from parted drapes. Same went for the rooms in the front block. The two lights that were still on were at the far end of the block; well beyond his destination. Similarly, all the lights in the reception building were off. It was raining heavily now; 'raining ropes' as the French would say, and when Dooks squinted out past the left edge of the front block, the single truck he saw passing in the street beyond the trees looked like a pixelated photograph with headlights.

Even before he reached his destination Dooks had already made one minor modification in Manface's plan: On his way back he wasn't getting soaked by walking in the rain; he'd reuse the walkway. He'd figured out that it didn't matter if his shoes got bloody, the rain would wash away all traces of blood, both on the corridor and also in the parking lot between the middle and rear blocks.

With that in mind, he quickly reached Room 13. He turned the doorknob and the door opened. Kudos to Manface.

Dooks stepped inside the room, which was garishly lit by candlelight, and quickly shut the door behind them. Then, while staring in disbelief at what the room contained, he felt blindly around on the wall beside him till he found the light switch, and then flicked it on.

Once the lights came on, Dooks realized that what faced him was a whole lot worse than he'd thought when the room was just lit by candles. His mind reeled and threatened to snap from what he was looking at.

"Manface wasn't kidding," he said aloud, while trying to understand exactly what had happened in here. But no understanding came to him as his gaze dragged between its two immediate focuses: the skeleton on the floor near his feet and the hole in the wall opposite, a bloody meat-lined hole that opened up into misty darkness beyond. The hole shrunk as Dooks stared at it, and as it got smaller, so it ejected chunks of mangled flesh and strips of skin into the room.

Dooks didn't move until the hole in the wall was completely gone. He didn't dare move. He was terrified that if he took a step in any direction, he would trip over a corpse or slip on some blood and fall into the wall, into God-only-knew what hellish dimension.

One thing I know is, I definitely won't be landing just outside this motel room.

The hole vanished, and only then did Dooks allowed himself to really examine Room 13. Doing so, however, made him wish the hole in the wall was back in place again so he could crawl into it to protect his sanity.

What the fuck happened in here? he pondered as he examined the corpses. *How did all these people die this violently without waking up the entire motel?*

But just like with the hole in the wall, Dooks had no explanation. The skeleton at his feet with four candles burning on its ribcage and spinal column; the headless woman at the far end of the couch whose head lay right beneath the spot where the hole in the wall had been; another blonde girl with a burning candle stuck in her back; and two other corpses, the man lying right in front of him and the woman on his left, at the foot of the bed—the beauty he'd noticed at the window; piles of viscera at different ends of the room. The smell of blood hung in the air like this was an abattoir that butchered human flesh for the devil's banquet table.

Insanity. I've got to get out of here soon or I'll go crazy too.

Dooks decided that the wisest way to approach the gruesome task at hand was to first locate the hearts that were already out of their bodies, or which (in the case of the skeleton lying at his feet) was already exposed.

He crouched by the skeleton and after blowing out the candles stuck to its bones, reached beneath the ribs and cut out the heart.

Manface is wrong. This never gets any easier. Even with gloves on, the feel of a person as meat was a nauseous one. Dooks felt it was okay to treat an animal carcass this way. To hold and wash a cut of beef, for instance—since animals were food. *But to treat a human body like this is just obscene. How the hell do coroners sleep at night?*

Once the first heart was placed in his black bag, he moved on to the man on the floor. The man was a weird sight to behold; his thoracic cavity was as empty as a new closet. Indeed, the way the dead man's chest had been opened up was eerily reminiscent of someone opening up a closet: from top to bottom, ribs, skin and muscle were folded back on each side like wardrobe doors.

Dooks avoided considering the puzzle of how this had happened and instead looked around to locate the missing contents of the man's body, which would hopefully include his heart also.

Has to be that bloody mess piled up below the TV.

He hurried over there quickly, and soon found the man's heart among the pile of organs. Once he'd severed it from its blood vessels, he placed it inside the plastic bag and crossed to the other side of the room to search for the beautiful woman's heart.

He stood for a while staring down at her corpse. He felt like looking at her face one last time; at that beauty that was now forever lost to the world.

In the end, however, Dooks resisted this impulse and didn't turn her over. He located her own innards beneath the window drapes and walked over there, with his attention temporarily snagged by a pair of paperbacks spilled on the bed, clearly while one of the dead women in the room had been emptying out their bag on the bed. It must have been a woman's bag because of the cosmetics and bottles of nail polish that lay around the two novels.

The two books were *The Bleeding Oysters* and *The Book of Atrocities*. Both were bestsellers by Drake Melville. Dooks didn't know much about the author other than that he seemed psychotic enough to have perpetuated this bloodbath Dooks was currently standing in.

Dooks reached the curtains and searched through the mess of innards below them for the beautiful woman's heart. He quickly located the missing organ, having now grasped the logic of human construction, how the heart always hung out with the lungs.

Once this heart was also safely stowed away in his bag, Dooks took a break for a short while. He sat on the couch and tried to relax; a king in a court of the dead.

He didn't rest for long, however; he was aware of the clock running down to daybreak and of the demon waiting for him in the rear block. And no matter how one considered it, being surrounded by the dead wasn't inspiring.

Okay, dude, back to work.

Dooks first tackled the blonde girl with the candle in her back. This was because the sight offended him. But after snuffing out the candlewick, he discovered that no matter how hard he tugged on the candle, he couldn't free it from her body.

After some consideration, and realizing that this was probably what Manface had also meant that it would be impossible to shift him from the couch he was on, Dooks gave up trying to remove the candle from her back. He pulled the dead girl up onto the coffee table like that, and opened up her belly.

It took him five minutes to cut out her heart.

And finally he was left with just the headless woman. She in turn presented a different kind of offense to Dooks, because he couldn't get over the feeling that her head was watching him disapprovingly while he moved her body up onto the coffee table in place of the blonde girl.

Of course this feeling was illogical, but seeing as nothing in this room of madness was logical, the fact that she might be observing him though dead made perfect sense to Dooks.

Dooks first tried to resolve his unease by turning the woman's head so that her eyes faced the wall rather than the room, but this didn't help either. In the end he carried her head into the bathroom and dumped it in the shower. Once he'd closed the bathroom door, he felt what he considered a normal lack of scrutiny again.

I'm going crazy, I'm going crazy . . . I'd better hurry this up before I wind up in a padded cell.

He quickly cut her heart out of her body and placed it in the black bag with the other four. Then he sat down again, this time to collect his nerves.

I'm about to walk out of this room carrying five human hearts. If anyone notices me and calls the cops, by morning I'll be famous around the world!

That was the one thing he didn't want happening to him; not when he was so close to achieving his goal tonight.

Once Dooks had gotten his nerve back, he got up and headed for the door. The rain was still coming down in streams, the thunder and lightning making enough racket to keep even angels in bed.

Relaxed now that the deed was done, and suddenly very amused at what the police would think when they discovered this mess in the morning, Dooks opened the door and stepped outside.

And found himself face to face with Christine Valona.

In his fright, Dooks almost dropped the bag containing the hearts; but a sense of self-preservation kept his fingers rigid on the plastic bag. He'd have immediately leapt back into Room 13, but the door was already clicking shut behind him.

"Hi, honey, how 'bout a quick blowjob?" Christine asked, stepping up close to him. "I guarantee it'll be the best one you ever had in your life." While propositioning him, her hands were freeing her breasts from the top of her blue dress.

Dooks stood there feeling paralyzed. *Oh my dear God, the mutt really wasn't lying to me! This lady really is dead!*

Now there was no doubt at all in his mind. It was her face that had just convinced him. Not her excessive makeup; but . . . for several seconds, he seemed to see the prostitute's skull through the skin of her face—bare bone, empty eye sockets, cracked and grinning teeth, pale worms writhing where her tongue should rightly be—and then she was once more very solid and very tempting flesh, offering her large breasts to him.

"Have a suck on them, honey, why don't you?" Christine enticed him in a heavy erotic whisper. "You never know, you might die before morning and then you'll really regret not fucking me tonight, won't you?"

But all Dooks now saw in Christine was death; death in an alluring female form; and all of the money in the world couldn't have enticed him to sleep with her.

"You know, baby, I-I-I," he stuttered while inching slowly along the wall in the direction of Hicks's room. "I mean . . . er . . ."

But Christine wasn't giving up. "Oh, come on, honey pie, don't be shy," she said, holding her breasts out to him and swaying her hips as she kept pace with him as he tried to get away from her. "Man, you're so cute I'll even let you fuck me in the ass without a rubber if you wanna."

"Oh yeah, girl, anal is sure to be really nice with a hot girl like you," Dooks mumbled, wishing there was a way he could scream out his fright without waking up the motel. Yes, at the moment the rain was super-loud, but he doubted it would be loud enough to mask the sound of his terror if he dared give vent to how frightened he felt now.

Dooks inched along further, and still Christine kept pace with him; offering herself to him. For a price that he'd already determined was his life. Dooks understood Christine's game. She had no true desire to fuck him. Christine still wanted his soul. She knew he was returning to Manface with the price of his life in the bag he carried, and that if she didn't stop him, he would escape her, and she was going all out to prevent that from happening.

Dooks's body screamed out to him to have sex with Christine, but thankfully his mind screamed even louder to him not to be stupid. Dooks refused to look at Christine's knock-em-dead figure and those devilishly alluring breasts, and instead focused on her disturbing face.

And then, once again the makeup and flesh melted away from her face and left just a skull atop her shoulders, a skull surrounded by long brown hair.

The skull laughed at Dooks and maggots poured from its mouth as it did so. "Go ahead, Harry, you win tonight," it said. "Go back to your demon. But remember, I'll always be waiting here for you if you want a nice sweet fuck."

Dooks immediately pissed himself. Then he turned and fled. Fuck having balls of steel and courage. At times like this courage was for fools.

At the end of the block, he looked back for a second before turning the corner. Christine still stood there—fleshless skull head atop female body—laughing at him.

Dooks didn't stop running again till he reached Hicks's door.

Then, once he was safely inside the room again, he emptied the bag of human hearts on top of the coffee table for Manface to eat, and then sank down on the floor beside the demon and burst into tears.

There was only so much even a desperate and brave man could take, and tonight Harry Dooks had taken about as much as he could handle.

Outside the rain beat down.

CHAPTER 19

End Game

The deluge of emotion that now consumed Harry Dooks prevented him from watching the demon consume the five human hearts.

This was practically Divine mercy, because afterwards Dooks admitted to himself that had he had to watch that, the sight might have driven him completely out of his mind.

But instead he sat there on the floor, purging his overwhelmed soul with tears, while his otherworldly companion filled the air with biting, slurping, and crunching noises that mingled with the beat of the rain, and gasps, moans and sighs of delight that didn't. The deluge of disturbing sounds flowed harmlessly around Dooks who sat safely wrapped in his emotional cocoon.

(Somewhere deep down, Dooks recalled that he'd just wet his pants and needed to change them, but this was a minor concern.)

Dooks felt his emotions normalizing at about the same time as Manface asked him, "Now, Harry, are you ready for your second wish?"

"Yes," Dooks said dully. "You know what it is, so just grant it already."

"Done. You can now expect to have a nice long life and die at home in bed as an old man," came the confirmation a few seconds later, which made Dooks, who was still sitting on the floor, now look up at Manface.

Next, Dooks leapt to his feet in surprise.

What the . . . ?

But compared to everything else that had happened to him tonight, what Dooks was witnessing now wasn't really odd. All that was happening was that the previously frozen dog was becoming itself again.

The transformation occurred swiftly, with the night-black statue on the couch suddenly growing brown hair. And next, the borrowed human face the demon had worn shriveled away and there was once more a dog's head on the furry neck.

However, neither faceless corpse in the room got its face back.

Yup, it's over, Dooks thought in relief as Brownie, properly restored, leapt down from atop the couch and headed over to him.

"C'mon, boy, let's blow this joint," Dooks said happily. "It's long past our time to be heading home." He figured the dog's restoration marked the end of everything here.

Manface just told me I'll live a long happy life, so that means I've no longer anything to fear from Christine Valona. I don't intend seeing her again anyway. Twice is more than enough. I'm going to sneak away from the motel the same way I arrived here, duck around the side of this rear block and fade into the trees. No one saw me arrive, no one will see me leaving either.

He noticed that Brownie was looking up at him inquisitively.

Poor mutt probably wonders what the hell just happened to him, Dooks thought. *Or maybe he's just confused that Robby isn't getting up from the floor. Nah, it can't be that; Robby was passed out drunk so many times that Brownie probably thinks this is just another one of those times.*

So he extended his hand and stroked the dog's neck. "Hey, come on, Brownie, let's get out of here. Nah, mutt, it's better you wait for me here, while I go get the money and then come back for you."

"No, we'll do it the other way," Brownie replied in a human voice. "You wait here, Harry, while I go get our cash."

Huh? While not taking his eyes off of the dog for a second, Dooks slowly backed away from it until his back hit the window.

"Yeah," Brownie went on, speaking in what Dooks now realized was Manface's voice, "even though Christine now knows she can't kill you tonight, she may pull a trick, hurt you in some way; and I don't want that happening. And besides, the money's really hers, so to get her to let go of it, I'm gonna negotiate a deal with her."

"How come you can talk?" Dooks finally managed to ask. He felt as if the world was about falling to pieces around him again. "Stop trying to drive me crazy, mutt. Are you Brownie, or Manface or . . . or . . . ? Which are you?"

Once more not trusting himself to remain standing, Dooks walked forward and sat down on the couch the dog had just vacated.

"Oh, it's a simple soul transposition," the demon replied. "The dog's long gone to doggie heaven; nice place—lots of bones to dig up and dead cats to chase around—while I am now here in its body; for good, I must add. So technically *I* am the dog now, except that I'm really myself of course—I'm still Manface. But that's confusing to me too now, since I no longer have a human face. What did you call the dog just now?"

"Brownie."

The dog nodded. "Brownie, right? Yeah, that's a nice name. Just call me Brownie, too."

"Whatever you say, mutt."

"So let me go get our money and then we can go home," Brownie said.

Dully noting the use of 'our' and 'we,' Dooks asked: "You're coming with me?"

The dog nodded. "Of course I am. I'm *your* dog."

And with that comment Brownie stared hard at the door which clicked open to let him out, and then walked off into the rain.

"Well, I guess it could be a lot worse," Dooks said once the dog was out of sight, then he reached across to pick up the unopened bottle of Wild Turkey 101 from the coffee table. He screwed off the top of the bottle and then drank from it while staring out into the downpour.

I'll need to find an umbrella before leaving here, he thought, to numb the other, crazier thoughts. *I'm a billionaire, and I'm going to live a good long life and . . . I've a talking dog? Well technically, it makes more sense to think of the new Brownie as a 'possessed dog,' right?*

Dooks was tempted to peek outside and see if he could overhear Brownie's negotiations with Christine. *Whatever can those two be talking about?*

But he didn't feel up to it. *Tonight has been just one bit of craziness after another; I'm good on the crazy for the next ten years.*

So he sat and drank his bourbon whiskey and avoided looking at the corpses in the room until the door swung wide open and Brownie walked into the motel room with Christine Valona behind him.

Christine had her dress back up over her breasts again, and was carrying a brown attaché case. On seeing her, Dooks almost leapt up in fright, but all Christine did was to set down the briefcase on the coffee table and open it up so that Dooks could see that it was packed to the top with stacks of hundred dollar bills.

That done, she smiled down at Brownie and asked, "Six months, right?"

"Yeah, six months," the dog agreed. "That's a stone cold guarantee."

Christine then smiled at Dooks also. And then she vanished; she faded away into thin air.

That wasn't the only vanishing that happened. Christine had been standing between Hicks and the coffee table. After she disappeared, Hicks did too. A quick glance to the left confirmed to Dooks that Robby's corpse had left the building as well. There was still blood splattered everywhere and both of their knives had been left behind, but no more dead bodies in the room.

"I don't know how much more of this I can take," Dooks told Brownie, before taking a long pull from the bottle of Wild Turkey. Then, when his racing pulse had slowed down a bit, he asked the dog, "Hey, mutt, what did Christine mean by 'six months'?"

"I made a deal with her that in six months you'd replace this million we're taking away with two million dollars," the dog replied. "I told her you'd put two million up where she took this from."

Dooks drank some more whiskey and asked: "What the hell does she need the money for? Christine's a ghost. She's fucking dead."

The dog shook himself, spraying rainwater over Dooks. "I dunno, but it's her money. She died to earn it, so we're gonna pay her back and that's that. . . . And anyway, in six months that two million will be less than chick feed to you, so what do you care? The only reason I bothered to get this for you tonight is so you'd know the ritual actually worked."

Dooks nodded. After a glance at the wall clock that revealed the time was now a quarter past four, he said: "Okay, Brownie, I guess it's time we left here," He'd begun feeling grateful to the demon for adopting the dog's previous name; it made rationalizing the crazy so much easier.

True to his word Manface/Brownie had gotten rid of the corpses, but Dooks saw no point in tempting fate; fate in this case being symbolized by police persistence. And so he performed a meticulous cleanup, packing his bloody clothes (both those he had initially worn here and his first set of borrowed clothes, which were now just as blood-stained) into a black plastic bag to take home with him. Robby's revolver went into the bag next. After which Dooks stripped off his gloves, washed both them and his hands, and stuck the gloves into the black bag also. Then he dressed in another borrowed set of Hicks's smaller clothes.

Once Dooks had gotten everything cleaned up and ready to go, it occurred to him that there might be an easier way to handle this than having to lug the bag of bloody evidence home and risk both being noticed by people or stopped by the police along the way.

He gestured to Brownie. "Hey, mutt, can you get rid of this bag for me?"

"Easiest thing in the world," the dog replied, and a second later the package of bloody clothes was gone.

The money-packed briefcase was still open on the coffee table—Dooks hadn't wanted to get blood on the bills. Now that his hands were clean he moved to shut the briefcase, but then paused.

First of all he walked off into Hicks's kitchenette and returned with some paper towels. Then carefully, so as not to leave fingerprints, he picked up the Necromantica spellbook from the coffee table, wiped the blood and demon-spit mess off of it, and then stashed it away in the briefcase's top pocket.

The spellbook still made Dooks feel uneasy as hell, but it worked, right? He had no idea when next he might need some magic assistance in his life.

Next he cleaned the blood off of the quarter they'd played the Devil's Coin Game with and dropped it on top of his million dollars. The coin had brought him good luck; he felt a sentimental attachment towards it.

This done, Dooks shut the briefcase. He snapped shut the clasps and picked the case up. He used a few paper towels to wipe blood off the underside of the case.

"Let's go home, mutt," he told Brownie after another drink of whiskey. "It's way past both our bedtimes."

Dooks found an umbrella and then they departed the room.

Dooks took the whiskey bottle with him too.

***

"How much farther to your place?" Brownie asked when they'd left the motel well behind them. "We've been walking for ages."

"Not too far now," Dooks replied, shifting the large umbrella so it covered the dog too, even though the rain was subsiding.

They were cutting through the woods on the south side of Carver Street. Dooks felt safer surrounded by trees, unlike earlier when they'd been walking beside the highway. Dooks was wary of being noticed by the police.

'Brownie' had assured him that there was no chance of the police arresting him tonight, or of them linking any of the deaths at the motel to him in any way, but he preferred to be cautious in case the dog was wrong.

"Okay, mutt, if you're going to be masquerading as my dog," Dooks told Brownie, "there's some things you'll have to know. Some rules you have to follow. I'm referring to the way you gotta act."

Brownie ran in circles around him, darting out into the rain to investigate the roots of the surrounding trees. "Yeah, like what?"

"Well for a start, no more feeding on human hearts. That's illegal here. From now on, it's dog food for you. Premium brand, top of the range, of course."

"Fuck that shit. I'll eat what you eat, man. McDonald's and hot dogs and . . . breakfast cereal. Can I at least have raw meat occasionally?"

"Whatever, mutt; I guess I can order sheep hearts for you, if you insist. Most importantly, though, you need to learn how to bark. Listen to the other dogs in the neighborhood if you aren't sure how to sound."

"No problem there." Brownie let off a loud bark.

Dooks gave the dog a thumbs up. "That's cool. Remember, no talking except we're alone . . . Don't ever try to pee or crap in the bathroom . . . take your canine ass outside. Yeah, and you need to keep wearing that collar . . . along with a leash when we go out." He shrugged apologetically when the dog gave him a pointed stare. "Hey, I'm not into BDSM or anything like that. That's the law."

"A collar and leash? Hey, I'm not your damn pet. You know, Harry, maybe I'll just run away from home."

"Be my guest. I'll try to rescue you from the pound before you're put down."

"This is complicated."

"You asked for it, mutt. Hey, I've been wondering about something. How the hell did you manage to transform into the dog anyway?"

"It had to do with the number of hearts you brought me from Room 13. I only needed one of them to grant your wish for a long life, so I used the latent power in the others to grant *my* wish—I wished to see the human world as a living creature, and, seeing as the two human bodies in Hicks's motel room were both dead, possessing the dog was my only choice."

"You're one smart mutt, mutt."

"And, Harry, stop calling me 'mutt' already. My name's 'Brownie' now."

"Yeah, whatever, mutt."

The End

ABOUT THE AUTHOR

Wol-vriey is Nigerian, and quite tall.

He believes there actually are things that go bump in the night.

He writes horror fiction—for adults only, please. And also some surrealist stuff.

Wol-vriey blogs at: *http://oddityfarm.wordpress.com*

WOL-VRIEY
BIZARRO AND TRANSGRESSIVE FICTION

BOSTON POSH (BUD MALONE #1)

In 2028 AD, the USA is a nation ravaged by hungry dragons and dinosaurs. In Boston, Massachusetts, private eye Bud Malone is hired to rescue a kidnapped heiress. But nothing is as it seems.

Malone works to unravel a tangled web involving Boston Chinatown, a 200-year-old woman with a 9-year-old body, white robots, a human-liver-eating psychopath, a golem, a porcelain dragon, and a snake goddess with a crush on him. There's also a woman obsessed with chicken sex. Then Malone meets Posh Lane, a gorgeous call girl who's desperate to quit her pimp.

Romantic sparks ignite between Posh and Malone, but Posh's past suddenly catches up with her in a BIG way. To save Posh, Malone agrees to run a quest for Earth's new rulers, the Forks. But, Malone has no idea that agreeing to the Fork's odd request will send him on the weirdest trip he's ever been on in his life.

BOSTON CORPSE (BUD MALONE #2)

MAGIC CAN BE MURDER! - Drag queen Lucy Tang is back in Boston, and is hell-bent on settling her vindetta against casino owner Sookie Ling. And suddenly, Bud Malone, PI, has the case of his life to resolve.

When Boston's robot police force are baffled by a mind transfer case, they come to Malone for help. The one person who can likely help Malone out here is the witch Soledad Bathory. But Soledad seems to know a lot more than she's telling him. It's a case not made easier when Malone meets Soledad's beautiful cousin, Josephine 'Slave' Bailey. Slave has her own plans for Malone, most of which involve teaching him BDSM and making him her new Master.

Oh, and Rick Rogers owes Sookie Ling a whole lot of money, a gambling debt that's going to be literally Hell to pay!

BOSTON CORPSE - Not your average detective novel!

Burning Bulb

WOL-VRIEY
BIZARRO AND TRANSGRESSIVE FICTION

BOSTON LUST (BUD MALONE #3)

"Bless it, Father, for she has sinned."

Seven murdered gay women, all their bodies completely drained of blood. All also with large parts of their bodies dissolved away like acid has been pumped into their veins.

Bud Malone has to find the female vampire preying on Boston's lesbian population.

Then Malone meets the beautiful Trudi Carmen and the case gets even more tangled. Trudi needs Malone's help in recovering a ring that's gone missing. But how in the world is one little black ring related to either the dead women or their killer?

Resolving this case will lead Malone deep into Lucy Tang's legacy The Abstracta. And then to the city of Genesis.

Boston Lust Just when you thought Bean Town was safe to visit again.

HELL DANCER

Six people find themselves trapped in Detention, a nightmare realm where the demonic Schoolmaster is hell-bent on reforming them . . . until they die.

Porn superstar Venus Deluxe came to Springfield, MA to party, and next found her life hanging by a thread. One wrong answer will mean her death.

Suspended BPD detective Tanya Rockford was trying to stop one kind of violence, but found a terrifying another. With her and her companion's lives hanging in the balance, it's going to take all of her courage and resourcefulness to escape this hell she's stumbled into.

Porn stud Chad Cannon has made a career from his ten-inch penis. Here in Detention, however, it's his brains that matter. He'll soon be hoping all the pot he's smoked over the years hasn't completely messed up his memory.

The three students, Sherri, Jordan, and Mike? They were all just in the wrong place at the right time. Will anyone survive Detention? . The evil Schoolmaster doesn't plan on letting that happen . . .

Burning Bulb
PUBLISHING

WOL-VRIEY
BIZARRO AND TRANSGRESSIVE FICTION

VAGINA MUNDI

Rachel Risk is a professional thief with super-strong hair that can stretch like tentacles to manipulate objects. Ashley Status has both a digitally augmented brain, and 'muscle-purses' in her arms and legs in which she stores inflatable objects—cars, guns, rocket launchers, etc.

When Raye is framed as the fall girl in a jewel robbery, the pair flee Chicago's vengeful robot gangsters and take refuge in the Hotel Bizarre, where the gorgeous 'vagina singer,' Femina, is performing for a week.

But the Hotel Bizarre is even stranger than its name suggests, and very soon Raye and Ash are involved in an deadly adventure, a struggle for survival the likes of which they'd never imagined possible with loads of deviant sex, drugs, music, and violence at every turn. And just what is the old woman in the skin desert really doing with all those cats glued to her walls?

VAGINA MUNDI—a Bizarro Hymn in praise of WOMAN!

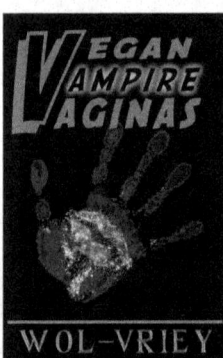

VEGAN VAMPIRE VAGINAS

The biggest bank heist in US history. And Tom Palmer can't remember pulling it off. And no, this isn't your standard case of amnesia. After a one-night-stand gone horribly wrong, Boston salesman Tom Palmer wakes up with a vagina implanted in his left hand. Then his day gets worse.

Tom is transported across space-time to a nightmare version of Boston, one where the Bizarro virus has transformed half the population into cannibals. Worst of all, Tom discovers that in this new Boston, he's the infamous gangster Pussypalm, wanted for robbing the Federal Reserve Bank of Boston a year ago. He also learns that the vagina in his hand is prophetic, i.e. it talks . . . after sex.

With 130 people left dead during his bank heist and six billion dollars missing, Tom knows he's living on borrowed time. It is in his best interests not to remember anything. Because once he does . .

Burning Bulb
PUBLISHING

WOL-VRIEY
BIZARRO AND TRANSGRESSIVE FICTION

VEGAN ZOMBIE APOCALYPSE

In the post-apocalypse worlderness, zombies rule the earth. They're allergic to meat, and brains literally make them explode. Zombies now eat blood potatoes, parasitic tubers grown in the flesh of humancows corralled in maximum security farms. Two fugitives meet in the ancient ruins of Texas. The first is Soil 15-f, a womancow who's escaped her farm a week before she's due to be killed and her blood potato crop harvested. The second fugitive is Able Kane, former head necros food technician, now sentenced to death for heresy. But Soil is no ordinary humancow.

Unknown to herself, she's the vegan zombie agricultural revolution, and the zombies desperately want her back. And the necros equally desperately want Able Kane dead. He's fled with a forbidden discovery which will reshape the world for the worse if used. And Able is just hardheaded/misguided enough to use it.

MELANIE NEMESIS CATCHPOLE

In Springfield, Massachusetts, Melanie Catchpole is hired to fetch back a magic teddy bear worth millions of dollars from a warehouse across town. Problem is, the warehouse is down in Springfield's O-Zone that totally weird sector of the city where Bizarro fell to Earth. The 'O' is a fairytale land, a place where dreams and nightmares literally live and breathe..

Worse still, the gingers—mutant cannibals—prowl the O. The gingers have already eaten everyone else Melanie's employers sent to get back the magic teddy bear.

Accompanied by the handsome but ruthless Doug Fisher (who she finds sexy but doesn't dare entrust her heart to), Melanie enters the O-Zone. Melanie and Doug are instantly caught up in an adventure they'd never have believed credible even if written as fiction . . . and Melanie's used to experiencing the very weird as the norm.

And now, additionally, there's a mystery to unravel: What does the dark, freezing-cold being called The Fixer want with Mary, the barkeep's daughter?

Burning Bulb
PUBLISHING

WOL-VRIEY
BIZARRO AND TRANSGRESSIVE FICTION

BIG TROUBLE IN LITTLE ASS

From Bizarro master storyteller Wol-vriey comes a truly weird western tale that will leave you awe-struck and on the edge of your seat...

In the town named Little Ass, tight-assed prostitute Rosa overhears a gunslinger's plans to assassinate rancher Edison Bennett. Once the badass Bennett learns of the plot, he ensures there'll be hell to pay for any attempt on his life!

Yes, it's going to take all of gunslinger Jude's shooting prowess, his eclectic collection of strange firearms, a trusty horse that requires an owners' manual, and the help of the lovely and invigorating Nell (who's EXTREMELY odd when the going gets weird), to survive the Bizarro hell that Edison Bennett unleashes in order to hold onto the land that he'd stolen from Madam Zizi.

BIZARRO 101 (A BASIC PRIMER)

Welcome to the strange place:

A collection of 37 flash fiction stories designed to introduce one to the Bizarro/New Weird Genre.

Weird, dreamy, nightmarish, absurd, sad, surreal, humorous . . . this collection of tales is all this and more.

***

"This primer is the very essence of any and all styles and types of Bizarro writing. Wol-vriey collects, distills, and bottles up these 37 tiny stories for your sensory enjoyment. This is an absolute must-read for anyone new to the genre, because it demonstrates the scope of what Bizarro is, and what it can be."
　　　　　　　　　　　　　—Teresa Pollack, Bizarro commentator and blogger

Burning Bulb
PUBLISHING

WOL-VRIEY
BIZARRO AND TRANSGRESSIVE FICTION

Dr. Orgasm

Courtney Taylor is young, intelligent, beautiful, and successful. She also has a boyfriend who loves her deeply. The problem is, no matter what Courtney does, she can't climax during sex.

When Florence Rigid's communist forces destroy the city of Metaphor, Courtney and her friends Teresa, Highball, Miki, and Heather are cast into the midst of a quest to find the only person able to save the land of Innuendo—Dr. Carol Orgasm, wanted by the communists for developing the O-Pill, a wonder drug that grants women sexual ecstasy on demand.

The communists will do anything to get their hands on the O-Pill and prevent its reaching the millions of Innuendo's women. But Courtney desperately wants that pill too. And so it's now a race between Courtney and the communists to find Dr. Orgasm first.

And Courtney has no choice but to win this race. She must win it: For her own orgasm . . . and for the freedom of female sexuality everywhere.

PUSSY TRANSMISSION

Pussy Transmission were the most decadent Pop Art ensemble of the 90's. Led by the beautiful painter Isis Lynch, the trio revolutionized the art world. Then suddenly, without explanation, Pussy Transmission vanished into historical obscurity. Now, twenty years later, three women come to Lynch Place. Lily and Nina are journalists desperate to interview Isis Lynch. Raven, on the other hand, wants to find her boyfriend, who's gone missing inside Isis's house. Raven's worried—she's heard that Pussy Transmission broke up because Isis began dabbling in black magic . . . with devastating results. All three women will shortly wish they'd never left home. Particularly once the rats in Lynch Place start warning them that they're going to die . . . and Raven meets Betty Butcher, the bouncy supernatural psycho who's intent on chopping her into bits. Pussy Transmission, Baby! Just because . . .

Burning Bulb

WOL-VRIEY
BIZARRO AND TRANSGRESSIVE FICTION

GIRLS ARE NOT SMILING
Welcome To The Road Trip From Hell

Pagan is demon-possessed.

Lori is suicidal.

Britt is just terminally pissed off.

Meet three young Boston women on the run from the law, each with problems that will fuse into more than the sum of their individual parts, becoming a holocaust of sex and violence and terror, a literal rain of blood and horror and gore and evil.

And if that wasn't already bad enough, Pagan's pet demon is slowly transforming her into something both unspeakable and unholy. Truly, these girls aren't smiling.

BLUE NIGHTMARES
Consummate EVIL is coming. It is relentless and unavoidable. It is Blue.

Jessica Schreiber is seeing things. Very horrible things. Since arriving in Raynham for what should have been a relaxing vacation, she's been seeing *The Big Blue*.

Jessica is smelling things too—dead and rotting things that she can't see. She is sure those dead and rotting things are dead people. Lots of dead people.

Jessica's worst nightmares will soon become her reality. Her reality will soon become a terrifying nightmare.

The tentacled residents of the House of Death have a lot that they wish to show Jessica Schreiber. They have a lot that they wish to tell her. But will she survive long enough to learn their lessons?

Burning Bulb

WOL-VRIEY
BIZARRO AND TRANSGRESSIVE FICTION

BRAINCHEW

It was supposed to be a simple jewel heist, but it went badly wrong. Chuck got shot and died.

Lance hid his friend's corpse in the Pleasant Street Cemetery. But that was a big mistake—there was something undead, something extremely hungry . . . something eXXXtremely horrible, buried in the Pleasant Street Cemetery.

And Lance had just woken it up.

They called the monster Brainchew because it ate brains. Human brains. And it preferred those brains fresh from the heads . . . of the living.

And now it was awake again, Brainchew planned on feeding big-time tonight. Oh hell yes, it did.

BRAINCHEW 2: OUT OF THEIR HEADS

After Tiff Hooper recognizes Josh Penham, the man who abducted her and kept her in his basement and abused her, she brings her three friends to Raynham for a night of well-deserved revenge on him.

Only things don't go according to plan.

It is never a good idea to leave a corpse in Raynham's Pleasant Street Cemetery. You run the very real risk of awakening what lies underground there. And that thing—Brainchew—is more horrible and more evil than anything the average mind conceives of even in its worst nightmares.

Brainchew is back! And this time the monster is extra-hungry. But there are plenty of delicious human brains about tonight, and Brainchew intends to eat them all before dawn.

Burning Bulb
PUBLISHING

WOL-VRIEY
BIZARRO AND TRANSGRESSIVE FICTION

DARIA: AN EROTIC NIGHTMARE

Even the best laid women can go wrong.

Daria Simpson is HUNGRY. She's HUNGRY for sex and bloodshed and death.

Shelly Parker just wanted to have a threesome with her boyfriend Craig and her best friend Erica. Everything was shaping up nicely for their weekend of sexual fun and games, until they stopped at the creepy Crossway Diner and met Daria.

From the moment they met Daria, EVERYTHING went wrong for them; and it went wrong in the most horrific and terrifying of ways!

Daria: Paranormal service has been resumed.

WET BONES

Greg is about learning the hard way that you don't mess with Aunt Grace.

Nine completely fleshless skeletons recovered in the Massachusetts woods. Two detectives on the trail of a horrible, hungry monster.

Broken-hearted Allie Jackson has a date with a creature from Hell.

Things are about to get well out of hand for everyone, and in horrifying, terrifying ways they don't expect.

Burning Bulb

WOL-VRIEY
BIZARRO AND TRANSGRESSIVE FICTION

MR. UGLY

When a rotting corpse appears and starts butchering Raynham's youths, there's really only one question that needs answering:

Is this faceless and rotting monster Peter Howard, or isn't it?

Problem is, Peter Howard died 15 years ago. So how can he possibly be back from the dead and murdering people with such relentless and incredible brutality?

Peter's mother Malicia, who's just been released from the lunatic asylum may have the answers to the crazy puzzle, but the two detectives investigating the deaths don't even know the right questions to ask her yet.

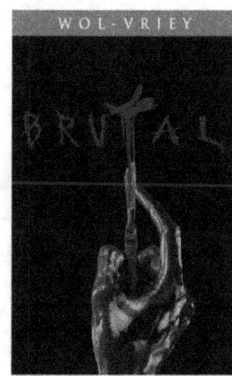

BRUTAL

Jane Winters is 28 years old.

She works as a checkout cashier in a department store. She's an attractive woman with a winning personality. She has both a photographic memory and an I.Q. of 189.

She's met the man of her dreams.

But she's also a cannibal with a unique and very scary mode of operation.

The group known as TULIP (The Urban Legend Investigation People) are out to either prove or disprove the legend of Insane Jane.

But have TULIP bitten off more than they can chew?

Burning Bulb

WOL-VRIEY
BIZARRO AND TRANSGRESSIVE FICTION

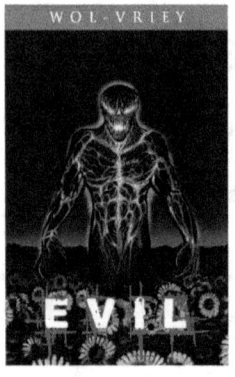

EVIL

The Evil began the week before Sylvia Stewart's 30th birthday.

Cathy Higgins died.

The Bargainer resurrected Cathy . . . for a price.

The price? Cathy's father Ronan had to plant some seeds for him.

But these were no ordinary seeds the Bargainer gave to Ronan Higgins. These were seeds from Hell: seeds which required human flesh as both soil and fertilizer.

And meanwhile, the unsuspecting Sylvia Stewart went ahead with the plans for her birthday party, which was to be held on Ronan Higgins' sunflower farm . . .

666

Ohio's State Route 666 stretches 14.7 miles between Zanesville and Dresden.

Most days, it's just a normal road with a funny name.

But for six minutes on the 6th of June each year, Route 666 becomes a gateway to somewhere else . . . a gateway to Hell.

Each year 13 unfortunates get trapped in the 666 underworld, with no way to get back home.

This year though, things are going to be very different. For one thing, there are currently a whole lot of turbulent human emotions at play in the underworld. And also . . . the psycho Al Gore is just about completing his collection of human heads.

And . . . what the hell is a church doing in Hell, of all places?

Burning Bulb

WOL-VRIEY
BIZARRO AND TRANSGRESSIVE FICTION

THE CLEAVERMAN

It began as a joke, a gag to pass the time that turned deadly. One rainy August night in Raynham, MA, nine friends jokingly invoke the evil phantom butcher called the Cleaverman.

These nine friends get a whole lot more than they ever bargained for. Because there's only one way to return the deadly Cleaverman back to the darkness he came from, and that is to solve his riddle, which starts: "Tell me the name of John Cleaverman's wife . . ."

And human beings being what we are, even with the Cleaverman out to butcher them all, our nine friends still manage to stir A WHOLE LOT of human misbehavior into the deadly mix.

At the rate they're going, it'll be a wonder if anyone survives THE CLEAVERMAN at all.

PERVERSE

When 21-year-old Heather Forrest accompanies three of her friends on a weekend trip up to Vermont, she has no idea what she's getting into.

Because, during a brief stop in the western Massachusetts woods, the girls get kidnapped and things go rapidly downhill from there. Soon Heather and her friends are fighting for their lives, fighting to survive the most perverted and impossible situation imaginable. And meanwhile, Hank Rollins is also in the woods, hunting the unholy monster that killed his wife and son . . . and he's hunting it with live human bait.

Oh yes, there will be blood. And there will be terror and buckets of gore also. And truly horrible atrocities will happen. Most definitely so.

Burning Bulb
PUBLISHING

WOL-VRIEY
BIZARRO AND TRANSGRESSIVE FICTION

THE VIRGIN

10 million dollars in prize money. 1000+ video cameras, lots of deadly weapons, 10 Suitors, 5 Virgins & 3 Hours . . . to keep your hymen intact.

Hailey Osborne wants to sell her virginity for a hundred thousand dollars. But then she's made an offer she really can't refuse: how about competing to win ten million dollars in a no-holds-barred underground game show, where all she has to do is remain a virgin?

There's just two problems:
1. Four other women also want that prize money.
2. There's ten suitors all contesting to take Hailey and the other virgins' precious hymens . . . by any means necessary . . .

But hey, it's just for 3 hours, right? How hard can it possibly be? Hailey Osborne is about to find out.

THE BOOK OF ATROCITIES

Bestselling author Drake Melville has been missing for three years now. Drake vanished after publishing The Bleeding Oysters, an epic novel that set new standards for depictions of sleaze and depravity and human monstrosity in popular fiction. On vanishing, however, Drake Melville left a message for everyone, saying he'd 'left town' to go work on his follow-up novel The Book of Atrocities. The problem was, no one could find Drake. It seemed like he'd vanished off the face of the Earth. And now, three years later, Drake has just sent messages to his ex-wife Liz, his current (and abandoned) wife Melody; and his younger sister Chloe . . . asking them to meet him in Raynham, MA. Drake says he's now completed The Book of Atrocities and is ready to present it to the world. But there's a whole lot that Liz, Melody, and Chloe Melville don't know about Drake's Book of Atrocities. And unfortunately they're on their way to find out those excruciatingly painful truths. Because, see, Drake Melville is a VERY EVIL man with a VERY EVIL plan . . .

Burning Bulb

WOL-VRIEY
BIZARRO AND TRANSGRESSIVE FICTION

THE FINAL GIRL

Here there be monsters . . . because we made them.

At a secret location, 8 young women assemble to compete on the ultimate reality/game show—The Final Girl. The 8 contestants are: A young wife and her grown-up stepdaughter, a police detective, a prostitute, a nurse, a school teacher, and unemployed twin sisters.

The Final Girl is a no-holds-barred show beamed to an audience on the Dark Web, a show where murder is permitted and mutilation is encouraged.

The Rules:
1. Avoid being killed and eaten by the show's monsters and bogeymen.
2. Find the prize money—24 million dollars in cash.
3. Hold on to the money.

But only 1 woman can win. And to win The Final Girl reality show, that woman will need to be even more bloodthirsty and ruthless than the show's monsters.

Have a seat, everyone. The most dangerous game is about to begin!

WOMEN

John Miller must die . . . TONIGHT!

Megan Kemp initially went to the Penderson Mansion to collect a debt. But from the moment she stepped in there, getting back outside proved extremely difficult. And then what had merely been difficult for Megan suddenly turned deadly. Because something was going on in the Penderson Mansion that night. Five VERY ANGRY women had a score to settle, and no obstacle on earth would stop them. . . . And no one would get in their way and live to tell the tale either.

"John Miller must die," the women had decreed, and it looked like the forces of Hell would help them accomplish their deadly aim tonight.

But as the night progressed, Megan, who was now trapped in a deadly game of cat and mouse in the Penderson Mansion, found that despite her own troubles, her biggest question was: "What the hell did John Miller do to anger these five women this much?"

Beware, folks . . . sometimes things really do go too far!

Burning Bulb

WOL-VRIEY
BIZARRO AND TRANSGRESSIVE FICTION

RATIO OF BROOKES TO ASHLEYS

After being cursed by a dying woman, Mike Broadman's love life completely nosedives. One girlfriend cheats on him and the next one dies a very messy death.

Next, a psychic informs Mike that he's under an evil spell that will keep killing his girlfriends, and that the ONLY solution (the ONLY way that he'll ever have a happy love life again) is for him to only date women named either Brooke or Ashley from now on.

Mike tries to comply with this, but still, the deaths continue, and now they're becoming even more brutal and bloody. Mike now finds himself in a race against time. He needs to 'equalize the ratio of Brookes to Ashleys' before it's too late.

And then, just when it seems things can't get any crazier or deadlier for Mike, he meets 'Brash' — the twins Brooke and Ashley Lawrence . . .

And the body count keeps rising . . .

DELICIOUS ZOMBIE

The zombie apocalypse happened two years ago. Today, zombies are mankind's new cattle. The undead are headed like cows and killed and eaten by everyone. The reason for this atrocity? Eating zombie meat has been scientifically proven to reverse human aging. Therefore, anyone who eats the zombies will live forever. Nowadays there are no old people anywhere on Earth. Everyone is young and healthy. Even deadly diseases have regressed. "

Digestion is Salvation," the Church of Zombie preaches. But three people—scientist Ethan Hackman, ex CIA assassin Paula Neyman, and socialite Zoe Patterson—seek to change this madness that is modern life.

With a group of ruthless and sadistic bounty hunters hot on their trail as they attempt to save the world, will Ethan, Paula, and Zoe succeed in curing the zombies, or will the age of the 'Delicious Zombie' continue? One thing is for certain, however; there will be a HUGE amount of murder and mutilation, bloodshed, violence and gore before the knotty issue of the zombies' food status is resolved.